A GHOST TOO MANY

J. THOMAS WITCHER

CONTENTS

1.

If she hadn't been so tired, she wouldn't have panicked.

At least that's what Jodi Weathers told herself.

It was understandable. It had sounded like a gunshot—a sudden, sharp crack shattering the morning stillness.

She couldn't be blamed for ducking down in her seat and violently yanking on the steering wheel. The realization that her every action was wrong came to her only as her back tires started sliding in the oily black water that covered the parking area of the Bayside Motel. Her heavy Ford Expedition went into an immediate tailspin, and she added insult to injury by slamming down hard on the brakes.

Hydroplaning. She knew better. Fortunately, she had not been traveling fast and she was brought to a shuddering halt when her back tires hit against the concrete barrier separating the parking lot from the muddy embankment leading down to what was left of Carver Beach. She ended up with her heart beating rapidly and facing the back door of the Bayside.

The kitchen entrance.

"Idiot," she told herself.

To end up half-buried in the mud would have been an embarrassing beginning for the new police chief of Sandy Shoals.

It was obvious what had caused the sound. The huge metal door that led into the Bayside Kitchen was standing open. There was still enough wind to push the door open with force enough to slam against the metal back panel that surrounded the door. The question was, had somebody jimmied the lock on the door, or was it a lingering result of the force of Hurricane Andrea?

Looters had been a fear all along. The three motels and the dozens of vacation cottages along Carver Beach had been hurriedly evacuated. Lots of valuables had been left behind. There were always people who would take advantage. Easy pickings.

She knew she had to check it out. There were some units from the sheriff's department out working, but she had been listening to them on her car radio and they were mostly in the far end of the county. And besides her, there was only one other officer remaining on the Sandy Shoals Police Force, and she had no idea where he was.

She felt reluctant to get back out in the drizzling rain. It shouldn't matter. Her clothes were soaked through. Three days of wind, rain and intermittent sleep had tested her endurance. Her body felt heavy—waterlogged.

She climbed slowly out of her car just as a man came bursting out of the kitchen door like a thoroughbred charging the starting gate. He was a small, stocky man, almost elfin in appearance. He appeared to be wearing every article of clothing he had ever owned, and none of it matched. He carried a black, bulging garbage bag over one shoulder, making him look like a homeless Santa Claus.

He skidded to a stop, surprised to see her there. Then he turned and started a rapid duck-waddle down the narrow path that led to the beach.

"Seriously?" she said.

She recognized him immediately. Every town had eccentrics, and Freddie Thigpen belonged to Sandy Shoals. He had mental problems, was a panhandler and a drunk, but people thought he was mostly harmless. She had never heard of him being a thief. She suspected what the garbage bag contained, but she couldn't be sure.

She knew she could catch him easily. She had run track in

high school and college, and she was running light. She wore jeans, a black t-shirt and a windbreaker she had borrowed from the fire department. She also wore a pair of Winnie the Pooh tennis shoes that were a gag gift from the University of Georgia campus police, but they were surprisingly comfortable.

She also wore a Savannah Bananas baseball cap, also borrowed.

Not the standard police uniform.

She started off after Freddie with an easy pace. Her muscles stretched. The heaviness eased from her body, and she felt a little better. She always did when she was running. Freddie was still heading down the path, toward the beach. She remembered there had been a wooden stair about a hundred feet farther on, but she had no idea if it was still there.

The savage storm had wreaked havoc all along the coast. Trees and power lines were down. Cars were half-buried in mud that was once part of the beach. Debris was everywhere. Beautiful Carver Beach had nearly disappeared except for a small strip of white at the water's edge.

She made up the ground quickly. He might have gone faster, but he kept looking back over his shoulder. She also noticed his shoes were untied, and he twice almost tripped over the laces.

A part of the wooden stairs remained, but it looked precarious. Freddie might have done better if he had started upward, toward the access road. Instead, he opted for the stairs. He made it halfway down the wooden stairs before he stopped. He dropped the bag on the steps and bent over. She could hear him wheezing painfully. He gave her another panicked look and he pulled the bag up to his shoulders once more.

She stopped at the top of the stairs. The wind caused the stairs to shake dangerously.

"Come on, Freddie," she said. "It's dangerous, and you're going to give yourself a heart attack."

He ignored her once again as he started down the remaining steps. The bottom two slats were broken in half, but Freddie didn't hesitate. He made an Olympic-style leap to land flat-footed in the mud. Then it became comical because Freddie's heavy boots sank into the mud. He tried to go forward, but he was stuck. He twisted and turned his body until his bare feet slipped out. He managed only a few more steps before he tripped and fell.

Bottles spilled out of the garbage bag. She should have expected it. Most of them were empty except for a few drops in the bottom, but Freddie gathered them up as if they were precious jewels. He got them all stuffed back into his bag and then sat back. He looked as if he might cry.

Jodi saw the quick, furtive look in his face and realized he was thinking about running again. There was no point to it. She doubted he had done anything more than walk in the busted open door of the Bayside. She wasn't going to arrest him for stealing a bag of trash.

"I'm not going to chase you, Freddie," she warned. "You run again, and I'll shoot you."

He looked as if he half-believed her. Then he grinned. "I don't see a gun."

"Then I'll shoot you the next time I see you," she said. "Promise."

He had a hard time tugging his boots from the muck, but he finally managed. He didn't try to put them on. He stood up awkwardly. He carried his boots in one hand and he dragged the garbage bag as he made his way back to the steps. He sat down on the first unbroken step and put his boots back on. He still didn't lace them up.

Probably a fashion choice.

2.

Jodi waited at the top until he reached her. She made him walk a few paces ahead of her. He had a ripe aroma—a mixture of alcohol and body odor.

A few hundred yards farther along the beach was the place she had parked her ancient Volkswagen Bug the day she had arrived in town. Had it only been three days ago? It felt like an eternity.

Her Volkswagen was gone. The surge of water from the storm had crossed the beach, climbed up the embankment, and crossed the access road.

The beach had been the spot where her vacation rental cottage had been. She had arrived late afternoon and decided to leave everything in her Volkswagen and jog to the courthouse. She had planned on meeting the mayor and getting the tour of her office. Then she was going to return, shower, unpack, and spend the rest of the afternoon lying on the beach.

The sky had looked a little dark and it started to rain before she reached the courthouse.

On the courthouse steps, she had been met by a petite, slightly overweight brunette who frantically stuffed a pair of keys into her hand and informed her that Hurricane Andrea had suddenly turned back toward the coastline. Ten minutes later, she was driving the former police chief's vehicle back out to Carver Beach to help with the evacuation.

It was still not supposed to be bad. Most of the hurricane force was supposed to go back to sea, but a tiny sliver of the storm, almost like a boxer's left jab, had struck the coastline.

The resulting surge of water had crossed the beach, climbed the embankment, and crossed the access road. It had destroyed everything in its path, including a vacation cottage, a Volkswagen Bug, and everything she owned. It now rested somewhere at the bottom of the Atlantic.

Her cell phone rang, and she answered it without looking. She already knew who was calling.

"Where are you?" Dr. Theodora Hamilton demanded irritably.

"I had a little situation," she explained.

"Stop wasting time and get here," Dr. Theo said, and rang off.

Jodi sighed. She was tempted to call her back but getting irritated with Dr. Theodora Hamilton was not a good career move. Dr. Theo had been dispensing pills, delivering babies, setting broken bones, and involving herself in the politics and crises of the county since before Jodi was born.

At seventy, Dr. Theo could have been retired but she still sat on the boards of the county hospital and Hamilton Bank, and she was a member of the Sandy Shoals City Council. Small, feisty, and full of energy, nobody messed with her.

It also helped that she was part of the Hamilton family. The Hamilton family was old money, distantly related to Alexander Hamilton and cousins by marriage to Atlanta's Woodruff family of Coca-Cola fame. They were considered one of the first families of Georgia. A Hamilton had arrived with Oglethorpe. Other members of the family had come over from the West Indies and settled along the route that would one day become Highway 17. Hamilton Textile Mills had spread all over the southeast. No Hamilton had ever served as governor, but the family had put governors in office. They were the closest thing Georgia had to a royal family. In fact, Dr. Theo's father had once been referred to as "the textile king."

A Hamilton had put up the first trading post at the intersection that was now Highway 17 and River Road. It had done a good business for many years, but then Sherman's soldiers burned it to the ground on their march to the sea. Years later, it was another Hamilton who saw the potential in the area around the secluded and pristine Carver Beach and had started buying up land. He put up a two-mile strip of shops and restaurants. He even had the name officially changed from the Shoal Community, which he thought harsh, to Sandy Shoals. And he insisted on everything having a pirate theme, maybe because he liked pirates.

It was too cute for a lot of locals who started wondering where General Sherman was when he was really needed.

She told Freddie to stop when she reached the door to the Bayside again. She examined the hinges and the lock. It was as she expected. Evidently, maintenance had been faulty for the back door. Sea air had started rusting the hinges and the heavy metal lock. Wind had done the rest.

Jodi stepped inside. She was in an enormous room filled with sinks and a long metal table. Puddles of water covered most of the floor. An overturned trash can was near the door. The room had another door at the far end, and it was closed and locked; it showed no signs of being tampered with. This was as far as Freddie could have come, and there was nothing for him to steal. The bottles in his garbage bag were from the trash.

She stepped back outside. There was not much point in trying to shut the door. There was no way to brace, and the wind would probably force it open again. She also doubted any looters could easily break through the inner door into the motel.

Freddie had backed away almost to the embankment. He shifted from one foot to the other. He clutched his garbage bag tightly as if he was afraid she was going to take it from him. Even in the wind and rain, his odor was strong.

"You are a lot of trouble," she said.

She felt a rush of sympathy for him, probably not how a hardened police officer should feel toward the town drunk.

The empty bottles of wine were worthless to anyone else, but he might get a few drops from them. She figured criminal trespass was the only crime he could be charged with, and she doubted even that would stick. He had done nothing but empty the trash. It wasn't worth the time to do the reports.

"I should lock you up for your own good," she said.

His eyes watched her suspiciously.

"Stay out of the Bayside, Freddie," she said.

He clutched his bag a little tighter.

"You can keep your bottles, but stay out of the Bayside," she said.

Freddie nodded.

"I'm taking some supplies to the church," Jodi said. "I could give you a ride. They've got hot soup."

"I've got a place to go," he said.

She figured he was lying. The closest place for him to spend the night was a homeless shelter operated by the local churches, and it was out on Highway 17. He probably had some makeshift shelter somewhere that he would take his precious bottles. It was sad, but there was nothing she could do other than arrest him. She already knew he had been in and out of jail a dozen times, as well as a few group homes and rehabilitation places. Nothing seemed to help.

"Get out of here, Freddie," she said.

Jodi watched as he wandered off in the opposite direction. She wondered if she should have arrested him. Somebody once told her she was going to have to toughen up if she wanted to be a good police officer. Maybe so.

But she wouldn't start with Freddie.

3.

Shoal Creek Baptist Church was one of the oldest buildings in the community. Originally a Lutheran Church established by missionaries to cater to early German settlers, it had changed hands a dozen times through the years. The Baptists had ended up with it back in the sixties, and they had added a kitchen in the basement and a large pavilion outside for dinner on the grounds. It was one of Jodi's favorite things about the church. The members loved to eat.

The building was solid white stone with a shale roof. It was built to stand against the seasonal storms, and it had lasted through a half-dozen hurricanes. There were deep scars in places, a result of wind and hail. Only one of the original windows remained, and the latest storm had cracked it. They would replace it, as they had replaced the others, with a heavy storm window. Jodi thought the building reminded her of an elderly woman, still proudly wearing her makeup and finery while looking a little worse for wear.

It was built on high ground, so the surge of water had reached only to the bottom steps.

Electricity was down all along the access road, but Shoal Creek had two enormous propane tanks that heated the building and provided gas for the ovens, but there was no water. Turning on the water taps produced a hissing sound and black bubbles.

Dr. Theo waited at the top of the church steps. She did not look happy.

Jodi shivered. Dr. Theo not happy was as bad as the hurricane. She was a small woman, barely over five feet in her stockinged feet, but somehow, she always seemed larger. Her hair was thick and white, and her eyes were an odd violet color, hard as obsidian. Never married, she claimed that most men were little more than a useless appendage and she could do without them, but Jodi always suspected it was more than that. There was some mystery in her background, perhaps unrequited love.

Or perhaps Jodi was being foolishly romantic.

"You took your time," Dr. Theo said accusingly.

"I mentioned I had a situation," Jodi said.

"The situation is that there are people here who still need blankets, dry clothes, and water. There's no time to lollygag."

"Is lollygag even a real word?" Jodi asked.

They stared at each other for a moment. Jodi looked away first.

Everyone was a little cranky.

Dr. Theo turned to give instructions to a couple of burly men who came out the door. The men were church deacons and one was a city fireman, the one she had borrowed the windbreaker from. They looked as worn-out as Jodi. Everyone had been putting in a lot of hours.

The trunk of Jodi's car was piled up with much-needed necessities. It was an assortment of blankets, clothing, and canned vegetables. There was candy for the children. There were a few magazines and books, and a lot of jugs of water.

Water was the most valuable commodity. This time, Jodi had driven almost to Brunswick to find a grocery store that still had water on the shelves.

Jodi started to help unload, but Dr. Theo put a hand on her arm. "You're worn-out. Go down and get yourself some soup. Try that brown bread; it's delicious."

Jodi didn't argue. Dr. Theo had a way of taking charge and

bulldozing all resistance. Dr. Theo's energy seemed endless, and Jodi had a pang of guilt at having been so irritated with her. Having her around was a big help. Yes, she did have an abrasive attitude, and she liked to be in charge. She had little patience for what she considered nonsense. She was more Martha than Mary, but that was a big help when you had a wide-eyed child with a broken leg, and the ambulance a half-hour away.

Jodi didn't mind being told what to do this time. She left the men unpacking her trunk, and she walked up the steps into the church. She made her way down a narrow stairway to the basement kitchen. She smelled the soup before she reached the door at the bottom of the steps, and her stomach did a little flip. She had been living on cheese crackers, coffee and soda, and she wasn't even sure if her stomach could take real food, but she was going to give it a try.

The ladies of the church had bread, pies, and vegetable soup simmering on the gas stove. Jodi took a large slice of the home-made bread with a dab of butter and a large bowl of the soup. She found a seat at a table where somebody wasn't sleeping underneath, and she put her plate down and then returned for a cup of coffee poured into a Styrofoam cup. She sipped as she walked back to the table.

A big guy slept on the floor nearby, wrapped up in several blankets. He snored as loud as Beethoven's 5th symphony. He was another of the city fireman who had been helping her, and she had to admit that even the cold, stone floor looked inviting. She could probably find a couple of blankets for herself and an unoccupied corner. She was tempted.

Jodi sighed and took another swallow of coffee.

She ate slowly. The soup was pretty good. The bread was even better. Her stomach didn't react violently, although there were a few embarrassing grumbles. When she finished the last of the soup, she thought of getting another bowl. She was still hun-gry, but maybe another bowl would be tempting fate. But soon, she was going to have to have a real meal. Certainly, what she had been living on did not complete her food pyramid.

Somebody stopped at her table. Jodi looked up to see a boy staring at her. She knew what was coming and dreaded it. Her fifteen minutes of fame was going to haunt her forever.

"Are you her?" he asked. He shook his head. "I don't think you're her."

"I'm not," Jodi said. "I'm not her."

"My friends say it's you, but I don't think it is. You're old."

"I'm twenty-five," Jodi said indignantly. "That's not old.

"But you're not The Dancing Girl," he said before going off to find his friends.

The Dancing Girl. She had been sixteen, and she and several of her classmates were on the Gypsy just outside the marina. Music was playing. People were dancing. But she was the one her classmate took the video of. She was at the wheel in a black and green one-piece bathing suit that complimented her fair skin. Her red hair was a lot longer then, reaching almost to her waist, and she was moving to the music as she took the Gypsy out to sea.

Her classmate put it on YouTube, calling it “The Dancing Girl.” It went viral overnight. It kept popping back up when she won the state championship in track and field, and later when she was a runner-up in college for the Olympics. She thought it was behind her, but some enterprising reporter had found it in the archives when the mayor announced she was going to take the job of police chief. It had been shown twice on the nightly news.

4.

She took the last bite of her bread just as Dr. Theo found her again.

"I think we're over the worst of it," Dr. Theo said. "How were the roads?"

"Passable," Jodi said. "There's an upside-down UPS truck blocking the turn-off, and there's a lot of junk still littering the roads, but cars can get in and out if they're careful. The town is in pretty good shape."

"Have you made it all the way to the end of the access road?" Dr. Theo asked.

"No. There's still a lot of water across the road farther up."

Jodi knew Dr. Theo was concerned about the oldest building in the area, a historical landmark. Blackbeard's Tavern was supposedly built by Blackbeard himself, but Jodi's father had suspected it was built by the same German settlers who had built Shoal Creek Church. There were similarities in the style, but locals preferred the more romantic version.

There was even talk of Blackbeard's ghost, Edward Teach, being seen walking around the upper stories at night.

Jodi shuddered. She didn't like thinking about ghosts.

"The soup smells almost edible," Dr. Theo said.

"It's good," Jodi said. "It's got lots of vegetables and a mystery meat. I asked the counter lady what the meat was, but she just winked and said it was best not to speculate. I don't think it's beef."

Dr. Theo laughed. "I'm glad some things haven't changed, like your legendary appetite."

Jodi blushed. She didn't think it was legendary.

"And you're still drinking your coffee black," Dr. Theo said. "Don't you know that makes you taller?"

"Not funny," Jodi said.

Everyone in Sandy Shoals knew fear of getting taller had always been one of Jodi's phobias. She had shot up like a weed in grammar school, and she had kept growing in high school. She was taller than everyone else. It made her dates few and far between. High school boys seemed to feel inferior dating taller girls. In college, the boys had started catching up to her height, but only a few.

Jokes about her height had always hung around her like a black cloud. Lots of people found her height amusing. She had developed a thick skin, but she still had cried herself to sleep more than a few times. How's the weather up there? What does a tall person do when they see a plane? Duck. Or her favorite: What do a tall wizard and a tall elf have in common? They both need a short hobbit to save their butts.

Somebody had written that joke on the front page on her copy of *Lord of the Rings*. She had never discovered the culprit, but that was probably a good thing. There might have been a few more busted noses, and Dr. Theo would have even more stories about Jodi's infamous temper.

"So, what was the situation you ran into?" Dr. Theo asked.

"Freddie Thigpen," Jodi answered. "I found him in the kitchen area of the Bayside. He was taking mostly empty bottles from the trash."

"Poor Freddie," Dr. Theo said

"What is wrong with him?" Jodi asked. "Besides, being a drunk, I mean."

Dr. Theo shrugged. "I wish I knew. There's just something wrong with his head. I wish I had the answers. Or a magic pill."

"That would be nice," Jodi said. "A magic pill to solve all our issues."

"Perhaps you could use one," Dr. Theo suggested

"If a magic pill could find me a hot shower and a place to sleep, I agree."

"You could always sleep at the marina," Dr. Theo suggested, a hint of anxiety in her voice.

Jodi shook her head. "No, I'm not ready for that. Not yet."

"Have you even talked to your father since you arrived?" Dr. Theo asked.

“I talked to him. Briefly. He says the marina got through the storm in good shape.”

The Weathers Marina was practically a historical landmark in Sandy Shoals. It had been first owned and operated by her great grandfather, grandfather and then her father. Everyone had expected Jodi to take over eventually because she seemed to have the same intense love for the sea and boats as her father.

Things had not worked out that way.

“A lot of marinas around here and Brunswick have closed down. Your father has sacrificed a lot to keep it running.”

She disliked the slight suggestion of accusation in Dr. Theo’s voice. It was true. Jodi’s father had dedicated his entire life to the marina. He was smart and had a good chance at college, but her grandfather had a fatal heart attack before her dad graduated high school. They buried him in the same cemetery where her grandmother was buried, and her Dad dropped out to keep the marina running. He continued taking adult classes at night. A month before his nineteenth birthday, he received his diploma and then married his high school sweetheart. He was not yet twenty when Jodi came into the world. By then her mother had developed the cancer that would eventually take her life, and from Jodi's earliest memories were of her dad constantly telling her to quiet down, her mother was sleeping.

Her mother died when she was six, but it was only later that she got a sense of her loss. As a child, she had known only resentment for the sickly woman in the back room who often kept them inside when she wanted to be outside.

"And Kate?" Dr. Theo asked hesitantly. "Have you talked to Kate?"

"No," Jodi said, resentment thick in her tone. "I haven't talked to Kate in a long time."

Kate. Once, best friend. Almost sister. Betrayer.

With a sigh, Dr. Theo took a folded piece of paper from her pocket and handed it to Jodi. An address was written on it in Dr. Theo's almost illegible handwriting: 221B Baker Street. From Jodi's memory, Baker Street was one of the narrow, tree-lined streets hidden behind the courthouse. There were only a few houses, and most of them were old and in need of repair. She remembered the streets behind the courthouse used to flood badly when there were storms. She also remembered there was a wooded park with hiking trails directly across Baker Street. Her high school track team had sometimes trained there.

"What is this?" Jodi asked.

"It's the address of a duplex on Baker Street. Most of the old houses, including this one, have been renovated in that area. They're much nicer. This one has hot water and a bed. It's the best you're going to find right now. All the motels for miles in either direction are full, and you'd have to drive to Brunswick or Gainesville for a room. We've pushed you hard enough, and I recommend a long rest."

"This is unexpected," Jodi said. "And much appreciated."

She had not really been looking forward to sleeping on a cold cement floor or going without a shower another day.

"It's the least I can do," Dr. Theo said. "You know, I was one of the members of the city council who wasn't sure you were right for the job of police chief. I thought you might be a little young, and I kept remembering that redheaded tomboy with the ferocious temper. But you've changed. You're a lot more mature, and you have a surprisingly good head on your shoulders. I've been impressed by the way you've handled yourself the last three days. I think everyone has."

The conversation embarrassed her enough that she immediately picked up her empty bowl and coffee cup and went to throw it away in the trash. Dr. Theo followed her.

"You'll have to pick up the keys from my grand-nephew. He's waiting at the courthouse, along with a bag I had your father bring. Kate packed up some of the clothes you left behind."

"You already knew I wasn't going to stay at the marina," Jodi said.

"I suspected it," Dr. Theo said. "I hoped for a different outcome. I thought five years might be long enough to stay angry."

Not nearly long enough, Jodi thought.

5.

Jodi did a last-minute check of the church. Outside, the rain still fell, and the wind was still brisk, but the real crisis was over. People were already on cell phones making arrangements. The first night of the hurricane, they had sat in the dark in the church and listened to the powerful winds, hoping the church would remain standing. They had spent a miserable first day, cut-off from help as the water receded, quickly going through what supplies were available.

By the evening of the first day, the water had receded enough for Jodi to make it into town in her patrol car, and church members had started showing up to take up cleaning and kitchen duties.

The church was still crammed with bodies, but at least the people were dry and fed. The kids were getting restless, getting into places they shouldn't be. People were asleep in the sanctuary, in the offices along the hallway, and in the pastor's study. There was even somebody sleeping in the dry baptismal pool.

Jodi thought it would have been a lot easier if people had only listened. The storm had struck quickly and unexpectedly, but there was still warning enough.

"Weathermen never get it right," had been usual answer, and some foolish people had stayed just because they wanted to see the storm.

Right. They were able to see it a lot closer than they wanted.

Jodi knocked on a bathroom near the front, but nobody answered. She had found out earlier the lock was broken, and it made for a few embarrassing moments. This time, it was empty, and she spent a few minutes trying to make herself presentable. Of course, the water was still not working. There were several gallon jugs of water on the floor, and she chose one to rinse her face off in the sink.

The view in the mirror was pitiful. She looked like a wet, bedraggled tabby cat brought in from the cold. It would have been sheer luxury to wash in hot water and to have a fresh change of clothes. Even more luxurious would be to wash her hair with real shampoo. Even though she wore her thick red hair shorter than usual, it still looked like a rat's nest.

"You're ready for the scrap heap, girl," she told herself.

Her clothes were not salvageable. She had worn the jeans and top for comfort on the drive, but they were already aged with rips and tears. They were not made for long soakings in saltwater. There were several unrecognizable stains.

Well, maybe she could get compensation if she was ever officially sworn in.

She dried her face off with a paper towel from the dispenser and dropped the towel into the overflowing trash. When she looked back into the mirror, she saw a man standing behind her. He had aristocratic good looks. He wore jeans and a university sweatshirt. He held an unlit pipe in his mouth. He seemed to be casually posing, as if he was about to get his picture taken or about to lecture to a group of nervous college freshman on the classics.

She was not as startled as she might have been. It had happened before. Perhaps thinking about Blackbeard's ghost had made him appear again.

"I really don't like your hair short, Jodi," he said.

"I know. We've had this conversation before. When you were alive. When your opinion mattered."

"You wound me, Princess," he said.

She shuddered. "Please don't call me Princess. And nothing can wound you. You're dead."

He looked a little puzzled by her statement.

"Why do you keep bothering me?" she asked.

She knew he wouldn't answer. Their discussions were usually one-sided and frustrating. He never answered a direct question. Most of the time, he simply looked confused. She had come to believe that he didn't know the answers or there was something preventing him from answering.

It was like talking to herself. Maybe she was, in fact, talking to herself, and he wasn't there. As Scrooge had once said, her dead ex-husband was probably a bit of undigested beef or a fragment of undercooked potato. More gravy than grave.

And she was nuts.

She had been divorced from him only seven months when he had died of a massive heart attack.

"You look tired," he said.

"I am tired," she said. "And I'm definitely in no mood for you."

"Just like when we were married," he quipped.

She sighed. "Please go away. Following me into a bathroom to talk to me is kind of weird, even for a dead ex-husband."

He looked around as if recognizing the first time that he was standing in the bathroom with her, and he simply disappeared.

Sometimes, it was that easy.

Jodi had never talked to anyone about seeing a ghost, but she had read a lot of psychology books. The consensus seemed to be that her ghost psychosis was a manifestation of some sort of guilt. Maybe because he had died so soon after their divorce.

She didn't think she felt guilty. If she did, her psychosis was deep down. Marrying him in the first place had been a stupid mistake caused by anger, hurt and vulnerability, but she thought her divorce was one of her better decisions. She was even more certain when all the crying coeds showed up at the funeral, bemoaning Professor Timothy Maxwell.

A lot of them tried to commiserate with her, as if they shared the same deep sense of loss. His colleagues said that his love of the classics and his gift of teaching would certainly be missed.

Sure.

His hobby of collecting coeds was not mentioned.

The first time he showed up as a ghost in her life had been at his funeral. He simply appeared in the empty chair next to her, in the same gray suit he was buried in. He seemed happy, smiling at everyone even though she was the only one who could see or hear him. He applauded all the many wonderful things said about him. Some were true. He had stayed with her all through the funeral and had ridden with her out to the cemetery. After his funeral, he continued to show up unexpectedly.

He told her once that she needed to move on with her life and forget about him

She responded that she would forget if he'd just stop coming around.

He only shook his head sadly as if it were somehow her fault.

She hoped she had left him behind by moving back to Sandy Shoals.

Evidently, it had been a futile hope.

6.

Jodi left the bathroom and walked through the sanctuary, picking a path through the sleeping forms. She stepped out of the church and onto the steps. From the top step, she had a good view of the Atlantic. In the far distance, a ship passed on the horizon. Looking at the ocean never failed to give her a sense of awe. She had forgotten how much she missed it. The old Brittany Fisherman's prayer went immediately through her mind.

Short and succinct. "Oh God, thy sea is so big, and my boat is so small."

Her father had taught her the prayer very early in her life to teach her to respect the sea and never to take its power for granted.

Hurricane Andrea had done some damage, but it could have been worse. Back in the fifties, Hurricane Ella had sent the water so far inland that it had flooded the town and reached almost to Highway 17. There had been even less of a warning about the storm's severity, and several people had lost their lives.

This time, the water had not gotten that far. Savage winds had torn off some roofs and broken windows. Cars had been damaged. There was only a little flooding in some of the side streets off Buccaneer Boulevard.

Carver Beach suffered the most. It was not a large beach, but it was well-known and popular. On one side, it touched the access road that crossed behind Sandy Shoals, and on the other side, it ended in dangerous jutting rocks. Beyond the rocks there was a wooded area. There were fences and numerous signs warning people to go no farther. The land beyond was beautiful but treacherous, part of the beloved marshes made famous by Sidney Lanier.

Signs along the expressway and along Highway 17 directed people to the turn-off to Sandy Shoals, “the friendly city by the sea,” and invited them to enjoy “the most beautiful beach in America.” The billboards had pictures of people frolicking on pristine white sands or enjoying the amenities of one of three motels or the many vacation cottages.

All the rental places and the few vacation homes were gone. Only wooden pilings remained, sticking up like forlorn sentinels out of the mud.

The mud was the worst part, covering the pristine white sand with dark muck.

Clean-up was going to be expensive and time-consuming. It would hurt everyone's pocketbook. The city had a few shoppers stopping on their way to Savannah, but it's finances mostly depended on tourists visiting the beach. Tourist dollars fueled the economy.

She went carefully down the slick church steps to her police car. The car was a nearly new Ford Explorer. It had all the police gizmos and gadgets, half of which she had no idea how to use. What she hated was that the former police chief had been a smoker, and it still smelled of stale cigarette smoke. Disgusting.

There were seven other police vehicles parked in the fenced-off area behind the courthouse. All were Fords. A couple showed long service. All of them had Chutney Ford stickers on their windshield. Chutney Ford was owned by the mayor of Sandy Shoals.

Coincidence? She thought not.

Jodi started the car and let the county dispatcher know she was back in service. She rolled down her window, letting the rain come in. Perhaps it would dissipate the stale odors. Her bath and bed called to her. She still felt a little suspicious of Dr.

Theo going to the trouble to find her a place to stay, but she was simply too tired to care.

She almost didn't see Freddie Thigpen this time. He scrambled up the embankment into the road ahead of her, waving his arms like a madman. She touched her brakes slightly, thanked the Georgia State Patrol for their wet-road driving course, and managed to slide safely to the side of the road. She stopped only inches away from what looked like the top of somebody's bathtub.

Her first inclination was to yell at him for nearly getting himself killed, but then she saw he was trembling, and his eyes were wide with sheer terror. He tried to speak, but his words came so fast, she couldn't make sense of them.

"Slow down, Freddie," she said. "Take a breath."

He still spoke like rapid-fire, but this time she made sense of them.

"You've got to come," Freddie said. "You've got to come right away."

He didn't wait for her response. He turned and started back down the embankment, shoelaces still flapping. She hesitated only long enough to call the dispatcher. She wasn't sure what she was getting into. With Freddie, he could have found a stranded ocean liner or a dead seagull, or something far more dangerous.

She had learned a few things through the years. It was always smart to let someone know where you were and what you were doing. That way, they knew where to pick up the pieces if something bad happened.

She followed him cautiously. A half mile to her left was the Ocean View Motel. It was the farthest from the beach, settled at the corner of the access road and Sandy Shoal's Buccaneer Boulevard. At the edge of the embankment, she stopped and looked over. Freddie was halfway down, and she couldn't see anything that could have frightened him.

She had no choice but to follow.

With no wooden steps here, she picked her way even more cautiously down the ice-slippery bank. One foot almost went out from under her in her first few steps. It would not be good decorum for the new police chief to go sliding down the hill on her bottom like a failed acrobat. Eventually, Freddie would recover from whatever had so terrified him, and he would be sure to tell someone. It would get some laughs from the VFW guys who met for the pancake breakfast at the Smuggler's Cafe every morning.

Rain trickled down the back of her jacket and made her more uncomfortable. There was not even a strip of sand in the area. The beach was dark and black except for a dash of yellow at the water's edge.

She stopped. The yellow moved gently up and down with the flow of the surf.

It wasn't a dead seagull.

"Stay where you are, Freddie," she said.

He stopped. Jodi was so tired that she was practically brain-dead, and she knew there were a dozen decisions that needed making. It was the wrong time to be making important decisions.

It wasn't fair. She remembered the mayor's words.

"I'm not looking for some sort of Neanderthal who thinks police work is breaking in doors and having a shoot-out with bad guys," he had told her. "I'm looking for more of a public relations type. I think you'd be perfect. Let the Sheriff's Department handle all the serious stuff."

Sure, Jodi thought.

And a dead body was serious stuff.

7.

The serious stuff. That was what the mayor kept telling her just a month before. Back then, the weathermen were just starting to talk about the hurricane season. She still listened to the weather reports from the coast, even though the sea was no longer part of her life. Sometimes, she woke up at night, thinking she was back aboard the Gypsy. She could almost smell the sea air and feel underneath her bare feet the different, subtle rhythms of the boat.

It was what she was thinking about when Roland Chutney walked into the campus police department at the University of Georgia. He was the last person she expected to see. Called Slick by family and friends, he was the recently elected mayor of Sandy Shoals.

Gus Hamilton was the former mayor. He had held the job for nearly thirty years. Slick's election had surprised her. The Chutneys were newcomers, not part of the elite. Slick had the money to buy into the exclusive Spirit Beach community where all the old families lived, but acceptance was a different thing.

Roland was a genial, smiling man, short, slightly overweight, and he had a fondness for expensive clothes and strong cologne.

Jodi shook his hand and knew her fingers would smell of his strong cologne for the rest of the day. No amount of scrubbing would help.

"Come to lunch with me," he said.

It was an odd request. They were not friends. She had met him the first time because he was a guest of Gus Hamilton on one of her father's fishing charters. She often went along as a deckhand. A scrawny teenager, she was all knees and elbows, and always oily from thick sunblock to keep her pale skin from boiling.

Slick later rented her father's boat for family gatherings or occasional business trips. She fetched and carried. She baited hooks, threw out chum, and sometimes handled the wheel. She made sure drinks were always cold and made sandwiches if called for. Some of the men complimented her and a few gave her tips, but if Slick said anything to her, it was in the form of an order.

His inviting her to lunch made her suspicious.

She shook her head. "I can't. I'm covering the phones today."

He grinned. "It's okay. I got permission from your boss. There's a steak place I want to try. It's called the Sad Cow. Billy eats there all the time, and he says the food is terrific."

"I wasn't aware your son attended the university," Jodi said.

"Oh yes," Slick said. "He's doing well."

Jodi gave a couple more excuses why she shouldn't go, but Slick was persuasive, like a used-car salesman, which was what Slick had started out in life doing. Curiosity made her give in. She wondered what he wanted. She wondered if he would have news of home. But the real convincing factor was the Sad Cow was one of the most expensive places to eat in Athens, and they had a tenderloin salad on the menu that was indescribably delicious.

Not to mention a baked Alaska dessert that was positively sinful.

Slick found a place to park near the front, and they were met immediately inside the Sad Cow by a very attractive hostess. She fawned over Slick as she led them to their table. She didn't glance at Jodi even once. Perhaps Jodi's campus police uniform made the woman uncomfortable.

"You say Billy eats here a lot," Jodi said, as they were seated.

"He brags about the place," Slick said.

"It's kind of pricey," Jodi said.

Slick shrugged as if the cost meant nothing, and it probably didn't to him. She wondered what it must be like not to have to worry about money. She wasn't a big spender but working for the campus police was never going to make her rich. It was sometimes a little painful to stretch a paycheck to the end of the month.

One thing was for sure, there was very little room in her salary for expensive tenderloin salads.

A waitress, just as attractive as the hostess but with dark, curly hair instead of blond, showed up to take their order. Jodi wondered if it was the food or the staff that kept bringing Billy back to the place.

Jodi ordered the tenderloin salad. The mayor ordered prime rib. They both had tea.

"How long has Billy been at the university?" Jodi asked.

"He's a sophomore now," Slick said proudly. "He started out with the idea of majoring in law, but I encouraged him to take a business degree instead. I hope he'll one day take over everything I manage. That would keep him close to home, and Sunni would like that."

Jodi nodded. Everyone in Sandy Shoals knew about Sunni Chutney—a statuesque blond who had been a swimsuit model for a department store catalog and had dreamed of becoming an actress. When her ambition to take over Hollywood or the New York stage had failed, she turned all her ambitions toward making her family a success. She ruled her home with the discipline of Attila the Hun. Slick obeyed her meekly. Her fourteen-year-old daughter was already the image of her, and Jodi doubted Billy had ever gone through any teenage rebellion. He was the physical image of his father but lacked his father's brains, energy, or salesman-like charm.

"He's met a girl up here," Slick said softly.

"Umm," Jodi said. She thought she was beginning to understand the lunch. Sunni was worried. She had sent Slick to Athens to find out what he could about Billy's new girlfriend.

"I'm not allowed to use the campus computer for personal reasons," Jodi said quickly.

It took a moment for Slick to understand, but then he shook his head. "Oh no. I just mentioned the girl. That's not why I've come."

Jodi breathed a sigh of relief, but she was growing more and more curious.

The waitress showed up with their food. The mayor's prime rib covered his plate. There was room only for the small metal cup containing his au jus. Bread, baked potato, and a small salad were served on side dishes. Slick took a bite of meat and then a bite of potato. He took a sip of tea.

"Delicious," he said. "Just as Billy described."

Jodi's salad was bigger than she remembered, and there was very little green in among the thick chunks of tenderloin. Her tea was sweet, just as she liked. Jodi waited for the mayor to tell her why he was treating her to lunch, but he was concentrating on his food.

"So, why have you come?" Jodi asked bluntly.

8.

Slick chewed, swallowed, and chuckled. He still didn't answer her question directly but instead asked, "How do you like working for the campus police?"

"It's a job. It has good points and bad."

"I always thought you'd end up working for your father at the marina," he said.

It was a sore subject, and she was afraid it would lead to even more painful subjects.

"Did you come to talk about my career choices?" she said abruptly.

"Yes," he said. "Exactly."

"I don't understand," she said.

"Have you thought about doing police work in another city? Like Sandy Shoals?"

"Not really," she said. "Look, I kind of drifted into this job after my divorce. I didn't set out to be a police person. I had my associate degree in liberal arts, and I was trying to decide if I wanted to go back to school. I needed a job in the meantime, and the campus police had one open for a file clerk. My boss convinced me to attend the academy just because some of the stuff I was filing was pretty sensitive, and I could make more money."

"And your boss said you did excellent in the police academy," Slick pointed out. "Near the top of your graduating class. You scored high marks on all the physical tests and you fired expertly at the range."

"I did okay," Jodi said.

"You did better than okay," Slick insisted. "And that's why I'm here. I want to offer you a job with the Sandy Shoals Police Department. We have several positions open."

"Several?" Jodi asked suspiciously. "How many is several?"

"All of them," the mayor said, looking sheepish. "Well, with the exception of one officer."

"All of them?" Jodi asked in disbelief.

"We were forced to terminate our entire police department," Slick said. "Even Chief Ballard."

"You fired Bob Ballard?" Jodi said.

Bob Ballard had been police chief of Sandy Shoals for as long as she had been alive.

"There were circumstances that demanded it," Slick said.

"What sort of circumstances?" Jodi asked.

"Just politics," Slick shrugged. "You needn't be concerned with the details. What you should know is that our city council met and unanimously voted to hire you."

Jodi did some mental gymnastics. Sandy Shoals was a small town, but they were tourist-based, and they needed a department larger than some small communities. Their responsibility also included the beach area. The fire department did the search-and-rescue work, but there was always a Sandy Shoals police officer stationed near the beach. There had been at least thirty officers working when she lived in Sandy Shoals. It was probably more now. And she had no idea how many administrative employees.

She also suspected the mayor was not telling her everything. Getting rid of an entire department had to involve more than simply a clash of personalities or politics.

"The Sheriff's Department is handling everything right

now," Mayor Chutney said, "but we can't allow that to continue. The county sheriff is very astute, and he sees a chance to step in and take over the city police. He's already making speeches about there being no need for a separate department. I fear some of our citizens are listening."

"Would it be a bad thing?" Jodi asked. "Might it not lower taxes?"

"Short-term maybe," Mayor Chutney said. "But within six months, the sheriff would be making noises about how his department needs more staffing if he is to police. It's happened before. Eventually, Sandy Shoals would be paying a hunk of tax money for something out of control."

"And the sheriff would be stronger politically," Jodi said.

"Exactly," Mayor Chutney said.

Jodi took a bite and chewed slowly. Then she took a sip of tea. A lot was going through her mind.

Jodi shook her head. "You're doing it backwards. What you need to do is hire a new police chief first. Get him hired and let him do the interviewing, etc."

"That's what we're trying to do," Slick said. "I guess I'm not making myself clear. The city council wants to hire you as our police chief."

She almost spit out her tea. It was the last thing she expected.

"That's insane. Your city council must have lost its collective mind."

"I'm serious, Jodi," he said. "And your boss says you can handle the job."

"You can't believe anything he says. He's the character that got me involved in this job to begin with. And I am going to have a long talk with him after lunch. He's not going to enjoy it."

"Your city needs you, Jodi," Mayor Chutney said.

She wondered how he could make such a statement with a straight face, but he was a used-car salesman turned politician. She braced herself for his sales pitch.

"Sandy Shoals needs you," he said. "And it's not like you'll be doing anything different from what you're doing here. You'll be hiring people, writing reports, answering phones. And the most important thing is public relations. You know how Bob Ballard was. He didn't understand how to treat tourists, and the tourists are our lifeline."

What he said made a lot of sense.

"It's where you grew up, Jodi," he said. You know the people, and everyone there misses you. I was reminiscing with someone the other day about when you won the state championship in the hurdles. We haven't won a track championship since you graduated high school."

"Who?" I asked.

"Pardon?"

"Who were you reminiscing with?"

He shrugged. "Just a guy I met at the Smuggler's Cafe. It doesn't matter. The point is, I think you would make a good police chief, and I'm certain the town council agrees with me. All you have to do is put in an application, and the job will be yours."

She felt the siren call of home tugging at her.

"And I know your dad will love having you close again."

Bringing her dad into the conversation was unfair, but it also didn't do what he intended. It only reminded her of the reason she had left. The food in her stomach suddenly felt a little sour. No matter how much time had passed, the bitterness remained. She couldn't escape it

"There are plenty of people more qualified," she insisted.

"It's home, Jodi," he said.

He kept picking at her homesickness because he sensed she was vulnerable. She looked away from him so he couldn't see the longing in her eyes, and her eyes fell on a man walking toward their table: short, stocky, with eyes set too close together and ears that stood out prominently. He looked misshapen. His arms were too long for his body, and his legs were too short, like he had been put together from spare parts. The best way to describe him would have been to say he looked like a Neanderthal. She had never met the owner of the Sad Cow, but she had read his name and description on several incident reports. He was an unsavory character.

He ignored Jodi and put a meaty hand on Slick's shoulder. Every short, stubby finger had a diamond ring.

"You're Mayor Chutney," the man said. "I'm Boris Petak. Your son is in here often. He brags about you. In fact, I recognized you from the newspaper article he showed me about you being elected mayor."

Slick straightened up in his chair, peacock proud.

The squat man smiled at Jodi, but there was no smile in his eyes. It made her inwardly shudder. As her grandmother was fond of saying, it felt like somebody had walked across her grave. More like stomping on it where Boris Petak was concerned.

"And we're always glad when the campus police come to visit," he said.

He spoke the words “campus police” as if they made a bad taste in his mouth. She didn't like the way he looked at her. There was just something creepy about him; not mad scientist creepy, but creepy like the guy on the street corner with a raincoat, and you knew he didn't have on anything underneath.

It made her curious as to how he knew Billy Chutney so well.

"Did you enjoy your meal?" he asked.

"It was perfect," Slick said.

"It's on the house," Boris said.

"I couldn't accept that," Slick said.

"Nonsense. Every politician I know loves a meal on the house. And I'm sure the campus police will appreciate it."

"I'll be paying for my own," Jodi said quickly.

Boris looked half-amused by her answer, but Slick quickly picked up on the tension between them. He might not have understood why, but sudden menace was in the air as thick as his prime rib. He raised a hand. "No. I promised Jodi I'd buy her lunch but thank you for the offer."

Boris shrugged. "Well, I tried. Come back again, Mayor Chutney, and bring your son."

There was no mention of Jodi.

9.

Yeah, right.

A lot of filing. Practically never have to leave the office.

It was time to call in the Sheriff's department.

Jodi tugged her windbreaker tighter around her, but she knew it wasn't just the rain and wind making her feel cold. She felt like an idiot for letting the mayor talk her into taking the job. She was out of her depth.

"Walk down the beach a bit and wait, Freddie," she said. "I imagine the Sheriff's detective will want to talk to you."

He didn't answer but he followed her directions. He walked a few hundred feet away and sat. He pulled his knees up to his chest and rested his chin and stared out at the ocean.

Jodi thought he looked kind of sad sitting there.

Jodi made her way back up the embankment. She called county dispatch and told them what she had found. She mentioned a request for a county detective. The dispatcher sounded bored. Probably the disembodied male voice belonged to a deputy who was used to finding dead bodies.

Every part of her wanted to remain in the car where it was warm and dry and where she could close her eyes for a moment. But she knew if she closed her eyes for long, she would be asleep, and it would take a lot to wake her again.

Reluctantly, she climbed back out of her car and made the dangerous journey back down the embankment. She knew enough from the few investigative tidbits she had overheard and from reading reports that the first thing to do was secure the crime scene. She wasn't sure it was a crime scene, but she was sure there was no way to secure it. A violent sea that could lift a half-ton pick-up truck and turn it upside down wasn't going to be leaving a lot of clues behind.

Not that she would recognize a clue if it bit her on the bottom.

She studied the beach but there was nothing to see but a few footprints the tide was quickly washing those away. And her instincts told her the woman had not fallen or been put into the water where she was. The tides would have moved her along.

Jodi had spent enough time sailing around the barrier islands to understand the tides. There were nearly 400,000 acres of saltwater marshes around Georgia's coast and they caused the tides to fluctuate rapidly.

She moved a little closer. She was already aware it was a woman, or a petite man with very long dark hair. The hair was moving with the tide, creating a sort of jellyfish effect around her head. A woman. Face down, she wore a skimpy yellow top and a short yellow skirt. There were deep scratches along the backs of her thighs.

And there was a grouping of colorful butterfly tattoos on her back. They seemed to be moving as her body moved with the water. They were really very good, different shapes, sizes, and the deeply etched colors were bright and vivid. They extended all the way across her back and down into the top of her skirt.

Oddly familiar somehow. It tugged at a memory. She took out her cell phone and took several pictures of the tattoos, without really know why she was doing it. Maybe some part of police training, long boring lectures, had remained in her subconscious. She stepped back and took some wider shots.

"That's called a tramp stamp," Timothy said.

She turned her head. Timothy stood a few feet away. He had

changed into a black bathing suit and had a towel draped across his shoulders. He looked kind of stupid standing in the drizzling rain.

"Not now," she said. "Please, not now. I don't need my psychosis bugging me."

"I wanted you to get one of those," Timothy said.

She remembered why the butterflies looked familiar, why it tugged at her memory. Back when she had been married, Timothy had tried to talk her into a tattoo. Just a small one. He had worn down her initial resistance and she had ended up going to the tattoo parlor with him. She remembered it was a female tattoo artist, a scary looking goth type. No way she was getting anywhere near Jodi with a needle.

"You also wanted me to walk around in six-inch heels and mini-skirts," she said.

"You were always a prude," he said.

"Just go away," she said.

She had seen dead bodies before, but mostly as a result of drug overdoses or traffic accidents, and mostly pictures. The real bodies she had seen close-up were cleaned up and in a casket. Like Timothy. He had looked handsome in his casket. She wished he would stay there.

She noticed the tide was starting to drag the woman back into deep water again. It was repugnant but she had no choice if she wanted the body to be around when the detective showed up. She gripped the dead woman by her arms and dragged her up far enough so that she was free of the water.

The woman had on one shoe. It seemed sort of odd. The shoe looked expensive, maybe a Jimmy Choo. She wasn't sure since she got all her shoes at Walmart. It was white, leather maybe. Lots of buckles and two straps firmly fastened around her, which was probably the reason it had stayed on in the rough surf. There were tiny pearls up the side.

A seagull gave a raucous cry. She looked up to see a single bird skimming over the water. As she watched, the bird caught a small fish in his mouth and headed upwards again. A late dinner. It made the soup she had eaten earlier feel heavy in her stomach.

"I can't believe you changed your name back to Weathers," Timothy said. "That's kind of insulting."

"Go away, please. I'm tired and this isn't the time to discuss it."

"It hurt me. It's like you were ashamed of my name or something. Think of how my parents feel?"

"Your parents never liked you," Jodi said. "I also defriended you on Facebook. How did that make you feel?"

"Such cruelty. What happened to the sweet innocent I married?"

"You taught me," she answered. "Now, will you please go away."

"We're soul-mates," he said. "We'll never be parted."

"That's what I'm afraid of," Jodi said.

10.

She closed her eyes and counted ten. He was still there. She tried ignoring him by concentrating on the dead woman. It could have been a drowning. She knelt in the sand. She noted bluish marks on the woman's throat. She held her hand over the marks and saw one of the dark marks on the left side of the woman's throat would have been the right placement for her thumb.

But she was no experienced investigator.

She stood again and looked around. There was no sign of anything like a purse or the other shoe, but she spent a few minutes walking as far as she could in each direction. She found nothing. Timothy walked with her.

"A nice romantic stroll on the beach," he said.

She sighed. Ignoring him was hard. She heard a car crunching on the gravel up top. A moment later a skinny man appeared at the top. He seemed a little apprehensive about getting too near the edge. He cleared his throat.

"You called in about a dead body?" he asked.

"Down here," she said. "By the water."

He cleared his throat again. "How do you get down there?"

Jodi tried not to sound sarcastic but failed. "You walk."

He looked around nervously. She knew he was trying to find some sign of a stairway, but if there had ever been one, the storm had washed it away. He started down tentatively, carefully testing each step as he came down the bank. He concentrated on not falling, and she could easily see why. The suit he wore did not come off a rack, and his shoes looked expensive and highly shined.

It seemed to take him forever to reach her side, and he was out of breath when he did.

"Detective Harold Blankenship," he announced pompously.

He was very neat. His dark hair was carefully styled. He was clean-shaven. He had a prominent nose and thin lips, and a complexion that looked as if he spent little time in the sun. She had wondered why he was not wearing a hat or a windbreaker in the light wind and rain, but it was as if he wanted to show off his appearance. There was a hint of vanity in his style and how he had introduced himself.

Something about him reminded her immediately of someone, but it was a few moments before she realized who it was. An actor on the old Any Griffith television show, a show as revered in the south as grits and good manners, had played a deputy named Barney. Harold Blankenship was the image of Barney except that Barney had been endearingly sweet and funny. She suspected there was little funny about Harold Blankenship.

She also sensed antagonism in his attitude, but she didn't know why.

"It was you that found the body?" Blankenship asked.

"No. Freddie Thigpen found her. I thought you might want to talk to him, so I had him sit over there, out of the way."

She motioned to where Freddie Thigpen had been sitting, but he had vanished.

"He was over there," she said.

"No matter. Everybody knows where to find Freddie. I'll get his statement later if it's necessary. Probably won't be necessary. Not for a drowning."

Jodi was a little surprised at his statement. He had not examined the woman but had only glanced at her casually. How could he know it was a drowning? She had expected somebody with experience, but Blankenship seemed not only inexperienced but disinterested.

"There are some bluish marks around her throat," Jodi pointed out.

He shrugged. Again, she sensed a strong feeling of antagonism. She didn't know why. She knew a few of the Sheriff's deputies, but she had never met Blankenship before.

His voice took on the tone of a lecturing professor. "I expect she's got a few bruises. Probably all over. Once you've seen as many drownings as I have, you'll understand. These are strong tides and bodies get banged around pretty good on the rocks. I wouldn't worry. If there's anything to find, the coroner will find it."

"In case the coroner finds something," she suggested. "You might want to take a few pictures. Maybe you could walk the beach a little, see if maybe you could find a purse or maybe her other shoe? I've already done that, but two pair of eyes, you know."

"Just a waste of time," Blankenship said dismissively. He looked at her a few more minutes. "She's missing a shoe."

Timothy laughed out loud. He understood her temper better than anyone and how she was struggling to remain professional and not give Blankenship a few well-chosen phrases.

She knew her words would be wasted.

As the comedian often said, 'you can't fix stupid.'

She took a deep breath. She heard another vehicle stop at the top. Two men holding a canvas stretcher came over the edge and started down. One slipped into the mud with an explosive curse. He managed to get to his feet and they both started down again. The second one slipped but kept his feet. The embankment was starting to become a slippery mess, and the cold rain was still falling.

"This is going to be a nightmare getting her back up," one of them said.

Jodi nodded in agreement. It was feeling even colder. She wanted a warm bed, or at least just to close her eyes for a little while. Mostly she wanted to block out the vision of the woman floating in the water.

It was a nightmare. First, getting her onto the stretcher and strapping her down. Blankenship could have helped but he didn't offer. He walked a little way down the beach and looked out at the water. Jodi helped the two paramedics by trying to steady the canvas litter as they worked their way back to the top. All three of them fell at least once, and twice dropped the litter.

Jodi breathed a sigh of relief as they made the access road. One of the paramedics thanked her as they pushed the litter into the back of the ambulance, and then looked with disgust at Blankenship who finally climbed back up.

Jodi watched the ambulance pull away. She thought about following it to the hospital, but she knew was asleep on her feet. She was going to find that bed She turned and found Blankenship blocking her path. He had finally lit the cigar and it was foul smelling.

"So, you're the new Sandy Shoals chief," he said.

"That would be me," she said.

"You must be somebody special," he said. "A lot of people around here wanted your job. I guess maybe they wanted a female. Affirmative action and all that."

She started to understand his initial antagonism. He was probably one who applied for her job.

"I'm sure that's the reason I was hired," Jodi said pleasantly.

His face darkened. She was forced to walk around him, but he followed her. He stood close enough for his arm to press against her as she opened her car door and slipped inside. In the Andy Griffith show, she remembered the character of Barney was given only one bullet and he kept it in his shirt pocket.

"Do they give you more than one bullet?" she asked.

She saw in her face that he understood her comment and didn't care for it. Because of his resemblance to the fictional character, it was probably not the first time he had been asked. At least she refrained from telling him what he could do with his bullet because it wouldn't be lady like.

11.

Only a half-dozen cars were visible as she turned onto Boulevard from Caver Beach Road. Most of the shops were closed. A woman was out in front a candy store sweeping up glass. She didn't look up as Jodi drove by.

The new courthouse was in the center of town facing the Boulevard. The old courthouse had been smaller, with less curb appeal. The new one had lots of glass, perhaps to give the idea that everything that went on inside was completely transparent.

Jolly Roger Lane ran off Buccaneer Boulevard beside the courthouse, and a second entrance to the courthouse was accessible by turning off Jolly Roger Lane into a fenced-off area behind an electric gate. The fenced off area had room for only a few parked cars, the VIPs. Other employees had to park in the city parking area two blocks away.

Directly across Jolly Roger Lane was the Sandy Shoals police department. It had also had a back entrance with a fenced-off area. At present it had nine parked patrol cars, a police van, and a bus. The bus was in a back corner and the tires had weeks grown up around it. It looked as if it hadn't been driven in years.

The building housing the police department was a single-story brick building that had started out as a couple of rooms and then been added onto several times in the passing years. If one looked from the sky the building was T-shaped with the bottom of the T facing the Boulevard.

Jodi had not been in the building since she arrived. The building had been locked and secured when the last fired officer left, and nobody had been inside since then. Her electronic card allowed her access through the metal gate into the parking area. The back entrance had a keypad. She tried the five digit keycode the mayor had given her, and nothing happened. She tried it again. It remained locked.

She was sure she had the right number. She walked around the front of the building and found the front had an old-fashioned lock. She had not been given that kind of key.

“Great,” she said.

It would have been nice to at least go in and look around.

She walked across Jolly Roger Lane to the courthouse. Lights were on in the front but there didn't seem to be anybody around. Everything felt deserted. A few of the office doors were open but they were empty. She thought she smelled coffee. Like a bloodhound on the scent, she discovered a break room at the end of the hall. A man sat at a table reading a newspaper. Her first thought was that he was not the man she was looking for. The Hamilton men were eerily similar in appearance, short, with dark hair and dark eyes. They tended to become doctors and lawyers, and seldom appeared in public unless they were perfectly groomed.

The man at the table was big and muscular looking. Even sitting down, he looked as tall as she was. Men who were her height had always attracted her, and she had also been drawn to men who looked slightly unkept, as if they needed a mother or a wife. The man at the table fit all her requirements. He had blond hair that needed trimming, and he needed a shave. He wore jeans and a white t-shirt that was paint stained.

She was surprised at her immediate attraction. She had not felt anything for a man since her divorce.

"Excuse me," she said. "I’m looking for Geoffrey Hamilton. He was supposed to meet me here with some keys."

He looked up at her with mesmerizing blue eyes filled with

good humor.

"Call me Geoff," he said, and laughed at the confused expression on her face.

"I really am a Hamilton," he said. "Honest. Grandfather Gus was so suspicious, he had my DNA checked. Theo says I'm proof that one of the Hamilton women had an illicit liaison with a pirate many years ago."

He stood. Jodi was right about his height. He was an inch taller than her. And he was not just tall. He was big, with wide shoulders and a massive chest. It was like being in room with a bear. He made her feel frail, which was rare.

And kind of nice.

"I was told to look for a red-headed Viking," he said. "You must be our new police chief."

She found herself responding to the warmth of his smile. There were some people you met, and you knew immediately you were going to be friends. Maybe there was truth that some people put off pheromones that triggered a social response in someone else. No real reason. Just chemistry. If it were true, Geoff Hamilton had pheromones by the bucket full.

"I'm not sure about that," she said. "I haven't been sworn in. I haven't filled out any papers. I'm sure I'm not getting paid. I can't even open the door to my office."

She knew she was blabbering like an idiot, but she was so very tired, and his physical presence was almost overwhelming.

"I can't do much about all the rest, but I can give you a place to sleep," he said.

She searched his face for a hidden meaning to his offer, but none was evident. It seemed as if she was growing more cynical with age, or perhaps that was a result of being a married to Timothy Maxwell.

“Aunt Theo gave me my instructions,” Geoff Hamilton said.

“She says I am supposed to deliver you safely to your front door.”

"That won't be necessary," Jodi said quickly. "I was born in Sandy Shoals. I used to run in Veteran's Park. I know Baker Street is right around the corner. It's walking distance."

"Sorry. Aunt Theo is she who must be obeyed."

"Oh, please," Jodi said.

"Write this down when dealing with Aunt Theo,” Geoff said. “The cost of disobedience is dire.”

Jodi smiled. "I'll remember that."

I'll get your key," he said. "And a bag that was left for you. I just made the coffee if you want some." He left her alone without waiting for answer, and of course she wanted coffee. She found a Styrofoam cup in the bottom of a nearby cabinet and filled it. The aroma made her feel almost human. She was not afraid of the coffee keeping her awake. Caffeine never seemed to bother her and right she was pretty sure she could sleep through another hurricane.

Just as soon as she found a bed.

12.

She had time for a couple of sips before he returned with a key and a worn familiar looking gym bag. It had been a gift to her from her father on her twelfth birthday. Kate had one just like it. Geoff gave her the key but kept the bag in his hand.

"I really appreciate this," she said.

"It's nothing fancy," he warned. "It's a renovated duplex. It has a few bits and pieces of used furniture, and there are sheets and towels in the linen closet. But the water heater is new. Lots of hot water. And there's a single bed with a pretty good mattress. You should be comfortable enough. You will have to put up with the neighbor who lives in 221A. You share the front porch with him. He's a nice guy, though. I think you'll like him."

He seemed serious about delivering her to the door. He told her to wait, as he shut off the coffee pot and tuned off the lights. He kept her bag so even if she wanted to leave, which she didn't, she had little choice. He walked through the hallway, and through a door and down a narrow metal stairwell, through the back door into the VIP parking area. A faded, antique Chevrolet pickup truck sat near the entrance. The bed was piled high with building materials. A green bumper stick read, "Don't laugh. My other car is a Porsche."

"You have a Porsche?" Jodi asked.

He looked confused for a half-second and then shook his head. "Nah. Just a bumper sticker."

She laughed. It went through her mind that Geoff could be dangerous for her. Men who made her laugh was another thing she found attractive. It had occurred to her often in the past few years that Professor Timothy Maxwell had none of the qualities she found so attractive. He was shorter than she was, and always neat, and he never made her laugh. The old expression was correct. Marry in haste, repent in leisure.

She climbed up into the pick-up. The seats were worn but comfortable. And thankfully, it didn't smell of cigarette smoke. Chief Ballard had smoked, and the patrol car still smelled of stale cigarettes. Even leaving the windows down had not helped.

"You say you can't get into your office?" Geoff said. "I thought it was coded."

"Yes, but the code doesn't work," she said.

"Eunice probably has the new code," he said. "Bob Ballard was constantly changing it. I wouldn't be surprised if he changed it when he left out of spite."

"I've been curious about that," Jodi said. "The mayor hinted Chief Ballard was fired because of politics but you usually don't fire an entire department because of politics. At least not at the same time."

"The mayor didn't give you the entire story," Geoff said.

"I'm not surprised," Jodi said.

"He's a little embarrassed. The entire city is. Our former police chief was arrested for being involved in a smuggling ring. The FBI came to the station one morning and escorted him out in handcuffs. Along with several of his officers. It turned out the entire department was involved, although some of them only in a limited way. Even the teenage girl working the reception desk in the courthouse lobby. They were all getting a piece of the action."

"What kind of smuggling?" Jodi asked, alarmed. "Drugs?"

"Cigarettes," Geoff said. "It was evidently quite an operation. They were bringing in cigarettes manufactured in other countries just the same way Al Capone used to bring in booze. Tax free. By the boatload. They then shipped to places like New York where they are so expensive. The first the city knew about it was when the FBI showed up to arrest Chief Ballard. Some others in the department were charged, along with the employees of a trucking firm that was used to distribute. Most everyone is pleading guilty and paying hefty fines. Bob Ballard and the trucking guy may have to serve time. Details are still being worked out."

"No wonder Mayor Chutney didn't want to discuss it," Jodi said. "It was a lot more than just politics."

"Oh, politics will come into it, especially with the current Sheriff. He wants to do away with the Sandy Shoals department. I'm afraid the Sheriff's department won't be much help to you."

"Again, not what the mayor implied," Jodi said, with a sigh.

"You have to remember the mayor is a used car salesman," Geoff said.

Jodi nodded miserably. More and more, she wondered what she was getting into.

The truck rode comfortably, but she knew if she closed her eyes, she would be asleep. It was only a half-block drive. Jolly Roger Lane dead-ended at Baker Street. The duplex was the third house on the left. Directly across the street was Veteran's Park, a wide wooded area that the city kept up. It consisted of a small pond and several hiking trails. It was a good place for a runner, and Jodi had spent a lot of training time there.

Geoff turned into the drive and parked the truck. She remembered seeing the house on the corner many times, and it looked nothing like it did now. A wide front porch had been added, and large windows in front. Another door had been added. It looked like a new roof. New siding.

"Someone did a lot of work," she said.

"I hate to brag," he said. "But I thought it turned out okay."

"Okay," she said. "You're telling me you did the work?"

"You sound surprised. Don't you think a Hamilton is capable of doing manual labor?"

She blushed. It was as if he was reading her mind.

"That guy that does the television home renovation thing. Chip. He's got nothing on me. I'm a wizard with my hands, or so I'm told. Then again, he's got Joanna so maybe he is a step ahead of me."

She had no clue what he was talking about, but then she wasn't into watching much television, especially home renovation shows. Now, if they were talking about repairing a boat, that would be different. She started to say something about Kate, who was a wizz with any kind of tool, but then she remembered she was still mad.

She opened the truck door and climbed out. Bag in hand, she looked up at him.

"Thank you again," she said.

"I'm not exactly leaving," he said sheepishly.

"What?"

He shrugged. "I warned you about your neighbor."

"You?" she said, after a moment.

"I'm afraid so," he said.

She wasn't sure having him so close was a good idea, but now all she wanted to do was find a bed. He gave her the key as they walked up to the porch. A couple of antique rocking chairs sat on the front porch and the side for 221B had a porch swing. She unlocked the door and stepped into a wide, spacious room with polished hardwood floors, high ceilings, and a large front window looking out at the street. A leather recliner sat by the window. A comfortable looking couch. An entertainment center with a television and a DVD player.

All the comforts of home.

"See you in the morning," Geoff said.

She shut the door and put her bag down by the chair. She slowly explored the rest of the duplex. Everything smelled of new paint. Two bedrooms in the rear but the smaller one was empty. The larger one had a bath and a full-sized bed. The bath had a tub and shower installed. There was a half-bath in the hallway and a small but functional kitchen. It came equipped with a Keurig coffee maker and a few K-cups of coffee and chocolate. There was bottled water in the refrigerator.

She found Timothy standing by the window as she returned to the front.

"What a dump," he said.

"I like it," she said.

"I think it's him you like." Timothy adopted a falsetto to his voice. "I love working with my hands."

"He seemed nice," Jodi admitted.

"He's not your type," Timothy said. "He's vulgar."

"Vulgar?" Jodi asked.

"No sophistication," Timothy insisted. "Probably didn't even graduate high school. Look at him. He's a thug."

"Go away," she said.

Timothy grunted and disappeared. She hoped he would stay away.

She found the sheets and towels in the hall closet as Geoff had promised. She put a set of sheets on the bed and took towels into the bath. At the last minute she remembered something she had intended to do earlier. She sat in the recliner and went through her cell phone looking at her pictures. She found a couple that plainly showed the butterfly tattoos on the woman's back, and she sent them along to a detective she knew with the Athens police along with a short message asking if he might recognize the artist. It was a long shot, but it was worth trying. The detective had been in Athens for many years.

She started to put her cell phone away and it buzzed. She was surprised that the detective was getting back to her so soon, but it wasn't him. She recognized the number and thought of not answering. She was so tired and would have preferred putting off any conversation. She might say something she didn't mean. Or something she did mean, but probably shouldn't say.

"Hello Dad," she finally said.

"I was wondering if you were okay," he said.

"Good," she said. "Tired."

"You sound it," he said. "Dr. Theo says you have a place to stay."

"Yes. A nice little duplex on Baker Street. Thanks for my bag."

"You are welcome here, you know," he said. "You always will be."

"I know, Dad," she said. "But I'm not sure how that would work right now. Probably not well. Let's give it some time."

"I see," he said.

He cleared his throat. She could tell he was about to say more, and it was exactly the conversation she did not want to have.

"I've got to go now, Dad," she said and abruptly cut him off.

She wasn't trying to be cruel. She and her father had declared a sort-of truce. He had come to Timothy's funeral, and they had met together a few times for lunch. But their meeting together was always awkward. Kate was never mentioned but the thought of her always seemed to be hovering about them.

She stretched out in the chair.

Thought about getting up and running a bath.

Closed her eyes.

13.

Jodi moved.

A small, protesting cry tore involuntarily from her throat.

For a moment she couldn't remember where she was.

She realized she had fallen asleep in the chair by the window. She was still in the same position as when she had fallen asleep, and every muscle hurt. She twisted awkwardly but couldn't make herself get up. Sunlight was in her face.

She stretched a leg out and pulled the gym bag she had dropped by the door when she entered the night before. Opening it, she found clean clothing and, even better, real shampoo and scented soap. There was also a folded note. She opened it and found it to be written in Kate's small, neat hand.

I miss you, was all it said. She crumpled the note up and dropped it on the floor.

She commanded her legs to work and somehow, she climbed from the chair onto her feet. Her knees felt rubbery. She measured the distance from the chair to the bath, and figured she had a small chance of making it. If she held onto things.

Good thing it was not a big house.

She went slowly, but she managed to get across the floor to the bathroom. She still longed for a long, sudsy bath but she sensed she had slept a long time and it was already late morning or early afternoon.

And she wanted coffee and she was hungry.

But then she was almost always starving when she

awakened.

She settled for a hot shower, and it felt luxurious to wash her hair in real shampoo instead of the bar soap available at the church. She felt almost human as she dried off. At least she could walk without support.

She went back into the front room in a towel. Feeling stronger by the moment and hungrier, she pulled on clean underwear, a pair of skinny jeans and an old sweatshirt with Weathers Marina on the front. She buttoned up her borrowed rain jacket.

The clothes she had been wearing were not salvageable. She picked them up where she had dropped them on the bathroom floor as she got into the shower. She stuffed them into an old laundry bag.

She dropped the laundry bag in a dumpster on her walk to the courthouse.

Rain still fell, and it seemed to have gotten cooler. She was thankful Timothy's ghost was not around. She had dreamed the night before and the mental images stayed in her mind. She had been out on the Gypsy with her father and Kate. Though it was a dream, she could still taste the sea air and feel the rhythm of the Gypsy beneath her feet.

The classmate who shot the video had dubbed her The Dancing Girl, but it was really the Gypsy that was dancing. The Gypsy was a twenty-five-foot motorized sailboat probably worth a hundred thousand new, before it was wrecked and left abandoned. The Coast guard had asked her father to tow it into the marina because it had become a boating hazard. It was possibly a smuggler's abandoned boat, and her father intended to salvage her but changed his mind.

For the next several summers, he, Jodi, and Kate had worked on her. A labor of love that bonded the three of them in ways that went far beyond family. She was an ugly, sluggish looking boat sitting by the dock, but on the water, she changed into something else. Like the ugly duckling turning into a swan, with the right hands at the wheel, she could gracefully skim the ocean.

But one flick of the wheel and the ungainly old boat would start plunging up and down like a roller coaster, threatening to roll over in the sea. Dancing on the waves, Kate called it, and it was an incredible rush.

She felt an odd disappointment to see that Geoff's truck was gone when she stepped outside. She told herself she was being foolish. She barely knew it. He could be like a sailor and have a girl in every port. The thought disturbed her more than it should.

From where the sun was positioned, it was later than she thought. She turned the corner and walked up the courthouse. The thought of breakfast and coffee tugged at her, but she wanted to check and see if the mayor had returned. Or if Eunice had a new code. Or maybe even some keys that would get her into the front door.

At least she would then feel as if she was accomplishing something.

Sandy Shoals was slowly recovering. A sprinkling of the stores had opened. All the protective plywood had been taken down from the windows. But there were few people walking in the still sprinkling rain. She tugged her borrowed rain jacket a little closer around her. The constant rain was getting more depressing.

The courthouse seemed a little busier this morning. A few of the offices had occupants. The front reception desk was still empty. She found Eunice Edwards sitting at her desk in the small anteroom. She had met the mayor's secretary only briefly and things were in crisis at the time, but Jodi had not gotten a good feeling about her. She was a hard, bony woman with a weak smile. She seemed out of her place in her job. She was not the person Jodi would have picked to handle important business, or to be the one people first met when they came to see the mayor.

Eunice looked up and gave Jodi a guilty smile.

"Yes?" she asked.

"I was hoping you might have the correct code for the back door of the police department," Jodi said. "I'd like to get into it sometime today."

Eunice reached into her bottom desk drawer and pulled out a small notebook. She opened it and read off a four-digit code which was the same number the mayor had given her.

"That's not the right code," Jodi said. "I've already tried that."

"Oh dear," Eunice said.

"Then how about a key for the front door?" Jodi said.

"I don't think there is one," Eunice said. "I never saw one."

Eunice seemed to be getting flustered at her questions. Jodi didn't think they were that hard.

"There's supposed to be another officer in this department," Jodi said patiently. "I've never met. He certainly wasn't out helping during the storm. Perhaps he's got the right code?"

"He's not available," Eunice said. "He's with the mayor."

"I see," Jodi said. "And where exactly is the mayor? I've been curious about that."

"He's in Atlanta," she said. "He had an important conference."

"The mayor left Sandy Shoals in a hurricane to attend a conference?" Jodi asked, in disbelief.

Eunice looked near tears. "It was an important conference."

Jodi took a deep breath and counted to ten. It helped a little. "Okay, then. Can you find me a locksmith or somebody in maintenance or maybe just somebody with a crowbar? Anybody who can get me into my own department."

"I'll try," Eunice said meekly.

Jodi was not filled with confidence. Eunice was out of her element. She was evidently one of those types who had trouble making the simplest decision. How she got hired as the mayor's secretary was beyond Jodi. She felt like she was accomplishing nothing with Eunice, but then accomplishing nothing seemed to be her major function as police chief.

And she was still hungry. At least she could eat. She turned on her heel and left the courthouse. She crossed the street to the Smuggler's Café. A low hum of voices greeted her, and the smell of eggs, pancakes and coffee.

Nectar of the gods.

Laughter came from a group of men sitting on the left side, taking up three tables pushed together. Some of them wore ball caps pointing out the fact they had served in the military, a lot of different branches. It was somehow comforting to see the men of the VFW were still meeting for breakfast. Classical music played softly from a CD player perched on the shelf above a painting of a boy fishing off a rock by Norman Rockwell.

The owner and cook, Max Childes, loved Beethoven and Norman Rockwell, Occasionally, someone might complain about the music. Only once. Max was an enormous black man with a shaved head, and a menacing attitude. It was not a good idea to interrupt his cooking with complaints.

To keep with the spirit of the place, Max dressed his employees in pirates' ensembles, some with eye-patches and short swords hanging from their garish colored belts, and even one with a fake hook for a hand. The fake hook thing had not worked, and now he simply displayed the book under glass, behind the counter, along with a lot of other odds and ends.

She ordered the complete pancake breakfast with coffee

and orange juice.

Her cell phone beeped at her after the waitress went to take her order, and she looked to see a text from her detective friend in Athens. A single word. Catnip.

No wonder the butterfly tattoos had seemed vaguely familiar. Catnip was the name of a tattoo parlor in Athens owned by an odd goth woman named Cat Esterhazy. Cat Esterhazy was a genius with the tattoo needles, and she had a passion for butterflies. The shop was where Timothy had taken Jodi right after they were married. He wanted a butterfly on her shoulder. Jodi had refused. The first of many arguments.

Jodi met Cat for the first time that day, but she met her several times after she joined the campus police. Tattoos weren't Cat's only passion. Cat also dabbled in herbalist medicines, and she sold a lot of them on campus. Campus police had picked her up occasionally, but there was nothing illegal ever found in her pill bottles. Some of her home-made concoctions were a little nauseous perhaps, but not illegal.

Her curiosity satisfied, Jodi figured she'd pass on the information to detective Blankenship although she was not certain it would do much good. Blankenship had already decided it was a drowning and she doubted anything could change his mind. Perhaps she should notify the Sheriff himself. Sooner or later she was going to have to meet him, another thing on her growing to-do list.

The waitress brought her coffee and orange juice. She finished off the orange juice with a couple of aspirins, and then sipped at the coffee. It was as good as she remembered. The coffee in the Smuggler's Cafe always seemed to have a sweet flavor, perhaps due to the delicious pancakes.

Her breakfast arrived. Scrambled eggs, bacon, and big fluffy, pancakes with blueberry syrup.

She took her first bite of egg just as Geoff Hamilton stepped in and came immediately to her booth. He still gave her the feeling of being near a big, shaggy bear. He carried a battered briefcase. It had taken her a few minutes to get one of the busy waitresses' attention, but the woman was at Geoff's side almost before he sat down. The woman was practically simpering as she waited for Geoff's order.

Disgusting.

Jodi was positive she had never simpered.

"Just coffee," he said.

She brought his coffee and Geoff stirred in milk and sugar He looked amused at her breakfast. It embarrassed her, but only a little.

"Aunt Theo told me you had the metabolism of a marine," he said.

She shrugged and took another bite. She had long ago stopped being embarrassed about her appetite.

"I was driving by on my way to a job, and I thought you might be in here. I wondered what you thought of the place."

"I liked it," she said. "It's nice. You do good work. It's also convenient. If I can just stay there a couple of days, until I find something else."

"You can stay as long as you like," Geoff said. "I already made out the rental agreement. I didn't think I needed to run a background check on the city's new police chief. And your relatives and my aunt all vouch for you."

"Shouldn't we talk price first?" Jodi asked.

"I think you'll find it reasonable," he said.

He took a folder from his leather briefcase. Inside was a printed rental contract with her name and information already filled in. She blinked at the monthly rental fee.

"This can't be right," she said.

"Too much?" he asked.

"No," she said. "I couldn't rent a boat slip at my father's marina for this amount of money. Even a small slip."

"It's a small place," Geoff said, shrugging. "And Aunt Theo says getting you a place to stay is part of our civic duty."

"Really," Jodi said, shaking her head. "I'm not sure I understand her sudden interest in me. Everybody in Sandy Shoals knows Dr. Theo, but up until the last few days I've never spoken more than a few words to her. Suddenly she's my best friend. It makes me curious."

"You sound a bit cynical," Geoff said. "I suppose a natural cynicism is part of police work."

"I'm not normally," Jodi said.

She still felt suspicious, but she wasn't stupid. She signed his forms, but she had no check to give him as part of the rental fee. Her checkbook was also at the bottom of the ocean. A trip to the bank was in order.

"I have a business question for you," she said, as she signed the last form with a flourish. "I'm trying to get a locksmith to get us into the department. Eunice is dragging her feet."

"Why?" Geoff asked.

"I'm not sure," she said. She hesitated and chose her next words carefully. She wasn't sure what kind of relationship Geoff might have with the mayor's secretary. Half the locals in town were related. She might be a great aunt or something. Or from her looks, a favorite schoolteacher.

"Eunice seems somehow ineffective," she said.

Geoff laughed. "A polite way of putting it. I've heard it said a lot harsher. But Eunice has some qualities that make her perfect for the job."

"What are they?" Jodi asked.

"She's related to Slick. A first cousin, I think. And she's not very attractive."

"Why should those things matter?"

"Because Slick is married to Sunni," Geoff said.

Jodi began to understand. Sunni's jealous rages were well known around Sandy Shoals. She seemed to believe every woman in town was after her husband.

"And it's a shame. The secretary before Eunice was ultra-efficient."

Jodi paused between bites. "Really? Ultra-efficient. That sounds like somebody who could help me."

"I'm sure she could. Her name is Frances San and she knows more about this city than anyone, including Aunt Theo and Aunt Theo sits on the city council. Frances was grandfather Gus's secretary for several years."

"Why did she leave?"

"Nobody knows. Some say Slick fired her. Some say she wanted early retirement."

"Could she have been involved in the smuggling?" Jodi asked.

Geoff thought a moment. "I don't think so. I've known Frances a long time. She doesn't seem the type."

"People fool us," Jodi said.

"I believe your cynicism is showing," Geoff said.

14.

Her idea was probably a bad one.

She knew nothing of Frances San other than what Geoff had told her, and it was possible Geoff's faith was misplaced. Frances San could have been let go quietly because she was involved in the smuggling, and Slick wanted to keep it quiet.

Or there could be a myriad of other reasons.

But it wasn't like she had a lot of work to do. She checked out the address of Frances San on her car's computer. The former secretary lived on Lullwater Drive in an area that had once been dominated by the Hamilton Textile Mill. The mill had still been in operation when Jodi was in elementary school, but it had closed her senior year in high school.

There was no trace of it anymore except a pair of rusted railroad tracks half-hidden by weeds at the turn-off and leading to a concrete slab in the middle of an empty field.

Driving past where the buildings had once stood made Jodi think of Kate. Kate's parents had both worked in the mill. They were both past middle age when Kate was born, born heavy drinkers, heavy smokers, and both already sick from the lung cancer that would eventually take their lives.

Most of the houses along Lullwater looked the same. They were ranch-style frame houses with large back yards and small front yards. Most were neatly kept. A few had overgrown yards and peeling paint. Frances's house was a white frame with recently painted shutters, and a neatly trimmed front yard. A small rock garden had planted shrubbery and a couple of ceramic gnomes.

Jodi still had no idea what she was going to say when Frances answered her door. Her visit was probably a waste but, if nothing else, talking to the former secretary might give her some new insights into how the courthouse functioned.

It couldn't hurt.

The woman who opened the door was small, with Asian features. She wore a snug green jumpsuit and tennis shoes. Her long dark hair hung to her shoulders and had a few streaks of white. Her eyes were wide, dark, puzzled.

"You're not Julie?" Frances said.

"I'm not Lisa either," Jodi said.

"Not Lisa," Frances said, puzzled but she caught on quickly. "Oh, the old song. You're not Lisa. And you're not Julie. Julie is my piano student. She's not very good, but her mother keeps insisting she take lessons. Julie would rather be out fishing with the boys."

"So, would I," Jodi said. "I'm Jodi Weathers."

"If I hadn't been expecting Julie, I would have known that right away. The former police chief's car in my driveway, and a tall, redheaded woman on my porch. You resemble your daddy. Dr. Theo said you might be coming around, but I didn't expect it to be so soon."

"Dr. Theo said I would be coming to see you?" Jodi asked. "I don't know how she figured that. I didn't know myself until a few minutes ago."

"She's Dr. Theo," Frances said, as if that was enough to explain. "Well, come in. I have a few minutes before my lesson. You want some tea or coffee or something?"

"Sure," Jodi said

Being around Frances San was a little like being caught in the hurricane again. Frances seemed to stir the air around her with her energy and enthusiasm. Two minutes after arriving at the door, she found herself seated at the kitchen table sipping coffee with Irish cream.

"And what can I do for you, Chief Weathers?" Frances asked.

"I wish I knew," Jodi said. "Things are a little confusing right now."

"And you've come to see me quoting the lyrics from sad old love songs and seeking assurances?" Frances asked.

Frances had a high lilt to some of her words that was almost seemed as if she was going to burst into song. It was pleasant.

"Yes," Jodi answered.

"You're also wondering if I was involved in the great smuggling caper." Frances said.

"To put it bluntly, yes," Jodi admitted.

"I'm not offended. Many people have wondered. The answer is no. I knew nothing about it. They hid it well from me, and that's hard to do."

"And yet you quit your job," Jodi said.

"One had nothing to do with the other. I quit because the town now has two mayors and I couldn't possibly work for them both."

"Two mayors? I don't understand."

"The day after Slick Chutney was elected mayor, a meeting was called for all courthouse staff. You know who presided over the meeting? Sunni Chutney. She informed everyone that she had some ideas for how to run the departments that would be much more efficient. She wanted to meet with all the department heads. And Mayor Chutney sat by her side looking sheepish while she ran the meeting."

Frances took a sip of her coffee. "After the meeting, I had a private talk with Slick. I told him it would be a cold day in you-know-where before I ever met with her. He said not to worry.

He would talk to her."

"He didn't talk to her, I'm guessing," Jodi said.

"If he did, she didn't listen. She was in my office the next day with a list of things she wanted changed. I told her that her ideas were not only less efficient, but some of them were just plain stupid. I guess I wasn't as diplomatic as I could have been. I might have hurt her feelings."

"You think?" Jodi said, trying to hide a smile.

"I don't blame the mayor. He's a good guy. But he's under her thumb. Well, maybe not her thumb. You've seen her, right?"

Jodi nodded. "A couple of times around town."

Frances held her hands out in front of her. "Like a playboy centerfold. I guess I could have gotten along fine with him, but Sunni thought she was the one elected. She started making my life miserable. I decided it wasn't worth and thought I'd try early retirement."

"I see," Jodi said.

"Nothing to do with smuggling or Chief Ballard, although I'm mad at myself for not knowing what was going on. Maybe if they had all been flashier, I would have noticed. But it's not like they were making a lot of money. They weren't buying penthouses or yachts. It was more like an extra steak dinner."

Jodi was silent for a moment. She found herself believing and liking Frances San. Of course, she had also believed Timothy.

But there was no question she desperately needed help, and Frances San was just the sort of person she needed. She hoped she wasn't making a mistake.

"And are you enjoying your retirement?" Jodi asked.

She shrugged. "Good days and bad days. I have my students, but sometimes I miss getting out. I miss being around people. The job was hard but sometimes it was also fun. It kept me alert."

"Did you know that before Chief Ballard left, he changed the code on the back door," Jodi said. "And nobody can get in."

Frances laughed softly. "That sounds like Bob. He was a practical joker."

"And a thief and a smuggler?" Jodi said.

"Yes," Frances said soberly. "A man of many talents. But why don't you just call a locksmith?'

"Eunice doesn't want to call one without first calling Mayor Chutney, and he is suddenly unavailable."

"I suspect it's Sunni she really wants to call for permission," Frances said. "If you like, I'll find you the number of the guy who does most of the maintenance stuff for the city. I'm sure he can get you in."

"I'd like you to do more than that," Jodi said.

"Oh?" Frances asked.

"I have not been able to hire one person so far. The sheriff's department is still answering our calls. It's a maze and I need someone who knows how to find their way through. Someone with insights into our court system works and the right people to talk too. I was promised a public relations type job. Instead, I've had a hurricane and a dead woman."

"Whoa," Frances said. "Back up. A dead woman?"

"Freddie Thigpen found her on the beach. The detective who answered the calls thinks she's drowned. I don't think so. There are bluish marks around her neck. I think she was strangled. But I doubt the sheriff's guy is anywhere near competent enough to do a thorough investigation. And me? Everything I own is at the bottom of the ocean. I'm not even sure I'm officially employed. I don't have a weapon, a uniform, and I haven't signed as much as a W2 form. I just used my credit card to buy gas for the police car. I'm supposed to have one officer and I'm told he's in Atlanta with the mayor. I'm thinking of getting on the bus and going back to Athens and beg for my old job back."

"It sounds as If you've had it rough," Frances said.

"Asking Eunice for a locksmith made me feel as if I was putting a strain on her ability. I need someone like you."

For the first time Frances seemed a little surprised. "You want to hire me. Dr. Theo said you'd come by to ask me stuff. She didn't say you'd offer me a job."

"Aren't you tired of giving piano lessons?" Jodi asked.

The doorbell rang before Frances answered. Shortly, Jodi heard someone playing chords in the front room. Frances poured more coffee when she returned.

"That's Julie. I'll leave her to practice for a while. Your missing officer is Hollis Bushnell. He's Sunni Chutney's younger brother. I don't know how qualified he is. Bob Ballard hired him even though there were several applicants ahead of him. Since then, he hasn't done much but drive Sunni around and run her errands."

"That explains a few things," Jodi said bitterly.

"To answer your question," Frances said. "I'm a little tired of piano lessons but hiring me might be a bad idea. Sunni was glad when I quit. It might put you at odds with her."

"Do I have the authority to hire you?" Jodi asked.

"According to our city charter, the police chief is in total control of the department. The chief answers only to the city council. Since you've been voted in by the council, you can hire anyone you want."

"Then I choose to hire you," Jodi said. "Please."

"Sunni is going to go ballistic," Frances said.

15.

Jodi thought she would make a tour of the beach area before heading back to the courthouse.

On the drive out to Carver Beach, Jodi found herself thinking of Dr. Theo. There was something there she didn't understand. She had known Dr. Theo all her life, but it had not been a close relationship. They had formed a kind of bond in the rescue work during the storm, but it still didn't explain the interest Dr. Theo was taking in her life. Dr. Theo had found her a place to live. With her unmarried grandnephew. Dr. Theo had mentioned her reservations about hiring Jodi as police chief, but the mayor had said the vote to hire her by city council was unanimous. Dr. Theo had known she was going to talk to Frances San, and maybe even guessed Jodi would hire her. It was almost Machiavellian.

But what really made her curious was Dr. Theo's sudden interest in Jodi's relationship with her father. What did it matter to Dr. Theo if Jodi called home?

Jodi turned it over and over in her mind, but she could make no sense of it.

Perhaps it would remain one of life's imponderable mysteries.

The upside- down UPS truck still blocked the turn-off and she made the detour through the parking lot of the Bayside. There were no obvious looters. There were still deep puddles in the parking lot. Farther on she found two power trucks sitting at the side of the road. Another was in front of Shoal Creek Church. There were also a few cars, with people packing up to leave.

The rains still fell as she stopped to go inside. The electricity was back on but there was still no running water. Half the evacuees had found places to go. A few remained still sleeping in corners. There was still simmering soup and coffee in the kitchen.

Water had receded enough for her to finally make the last mile down the access road to check on Blackbeard's Tavern. Another power truck was in front of the Ocean View Motel as she passed. A wrecked pickup truck blocked the road partially, but she easily went around. Two cars were parked in front of the tavern.

The tavern had changed hands several times during the years, and it was now owned and managed by a man named Hal Bishop, a California native who had married a local girl. At first people had not cared much for Hal. He had long hair and a beard, and he wore beads. Someone said they had seen him doing some sort of chant like a hippie. The truth was that the locals didn't want an outsider buying up what they considered their history. Blackbeard's Tavern, his ghost, his legend, belonged to them, not some California pseudo-hippie.

It didn't even help that he married a local girl, considering the local girl was almost as strange as he was.

It was doubtful Hal Bishop could have made a success of Blackbeard's Tavern except that he was a culinary genius.

The locals adopted Hal the moment they tasted his food. Instead of strange, he became eccentric.

Hal could make hamburger steak taste like sirloin, but his specialty was seafood. On his menu he had crab cakes that were unbelievable, oysters with apple ginger relish, a sea trout with wine sauce and lemon, and an incredible lobster soup.

He also did an exotic fish sandwich with cheese and zest spices. Along with spicy fries, it was one of Jodi's favorite meals.

Nobody ever asked exactly what type of fish was in the sandwich, and Jodi didn't care. It was that good.

The building itself was two stories and gray stone, with huge safety windows in front. The gravel parking lot was a little soggy. There was a small sign over the entrance but there had also been an enormous neon sign of a pirate waving his cutlass. It had been at the top of a metal pole.

The sign was gone. Only the pole remained.

Jodi got out of her car while Hal came around the corner of the building, waving his arms. He wore some sort of long red thing that looked like a choir robe and he looked as if he had gotten shaggier since she had seen him last. He waved his arms at her and she had a flashback to Freddie Thigpen showing up to tell her about the dead woman. She hoped there was no more dead bodies.

Hal came a shuddering halt in front her, and then looked surprised when she stepped out of the car.

"I thought you were chief Ballard," he said. "I was getting ready to call."

"I guess you haven't been keeping up with current events," Jodi said. "He's not chief anymore. It's a long story for another time. What's wrong?"

"Somebody broke in," he said. "From the back. Bianca says someone is still inside."

"Where is Bianca?" Jodi asked.

"She's in the back. Keeping watch."

Jodi didn't ask why he had left his wife in the back. Anybody who knew Bianca would understand.

Bianca stood in the rear by a broken window. She had one hand pressed against the window as if she was feeling a heart-beat. She wore an off-white Caftan with a black onyx necklace around her neck, and a red turban. She was almost as tall as Jodi and thin. She had dark eyes and beautiful long curling eyelashes that did not seem to belong to her angular face.

"They are still in here," she announced.

"And you know this how?" Jodi asked.

"You know that I am a medium," she said. "I can feel their presence. And my spirit guide agrees."

"Yeah, sure," Jodi said.

Half the time she had little idea what Bianca was talking about, but she couldn't point any fingers. Bianca had a spirit guide. Jodi had the ghost of an ex-husband.

Jodi looked a little closer at the window. It was not just the glass panes broken. The frame of the window had been ripped out, making a space wide enough for someone to crawl through. Nearby was a large piece of plywood leaning against the building. Jodi examined it a little closer. The plywood had four wood screws at each end. Cal had evidently put it up over the window, screwing it to the wood frame. Someone had obviously taken it down. Hurricanes didn't usually unscrew screws.

She started wishing her Glock wasn't at the bottom of the ocean.

Jodi thought for a moment about calling the county dispatch and asking for an officer to back her up, but she was afraid they would send Blankenship. Her head was starting to hurt, and she didn't think she could face him again so soon.

"Open it up," Jodi said. "I'll check it out."

16.

Cal opened the back door near the window, and Jodi peered inside. It was pitch dark.

"Got to get my flashlight," she said.

She returned to the car and got a flashlight out of the emergency equipment in the back. She debated again calling for backup, but instead patted her jacket to make sure she still had her cell phone.

She returned to the rear of the tavern and peered inside. The flashlight showed mostly shadows. Heart pounding, she moved inside and yelped when Cal flipped the electric switch on the wall and the area was flooded with bright light.

Evidently the county guys had gotten the electricity working.

She became aware she was standing in glass. She looked down and there was glass all over the floor. A dozen broken wine bottles were piled up in the corner.

There was also a terrible smell that recognized almost immediately. Bad fish. She moved over and glanced at the gigantic floor freezer. The lid was back. Fish, meat, and frozen vegetables were going bad. In the far corner of the freezer ice cream had melted into watery slush.

"Did you leave the freezer open?" Jodi asked.

"Of course not," Cal said.

It didn't make sense. If the freezer had remained closed, the refrigeration might have lasted a couple of days. At least some of the ice cream might have been saved.

Bianca made a sound of disgust and turned on her heel and rushed back outside. Jodi could hear sounds of gagging. Bianca's spirit guide must not have warned her how sickening the place smelled.

It was getting harder and harder to find a good spirit guide.

"You can stay here if you like," she told Cal, but she felt him walking close behind her as she pushed through the swinging doors into the main part of the restaurant. The stench of booze was worse than she could have imagined. Broken bottles were everyone. Someone had tried to make a fire on the concrete floor and there were burnt pieces of furniture piled up.

"Someone had quite a party," Jodi said.

"Why?" Cal asked. He sounded as if he was going to cry. "Why would somebody do this? They didn't have to break everything."

"Will insurance cover things?" Jodi asked.

Cal shrugged. "I guess. But it will still cost me. Premiums will go up. Maybe I ought to sell the place. I don't know if it's worth it anymore."

Jodi touched his arm. "I know it's really tough to look at, but don't make any rash decisions. Give yourself time. Think of it as natural storm damage."

She wondered if she was really trying to comfort him, or if she was being selfish. She hadn't had one of his fish sandwiches in over five years and she had been looking forward to it.

They both heard the noise at the same time. It sounded almost like somebody snoring, and it sounded as if it was coming from the back, from the bathrooms.

The smell of booze seemed even more nauseating as she moved through the serving area to the back hallway. The men's room door was held open by a green trashcan. She heard the sound again. She stepped into the bathroom and nearly tripped over someone.

A young man lay stretched across the floor. He was alive because she could hear him breathing. She moved closer and recognized him. His head was bloody, and she could see a few pieces of glass clinging to his hair.

And she knew her week had gotten a lot worse.

"Isn't that Billy Chutney?" Cal asked. "The mayor's son?"

"Yes," Jodi said.

"He's drunk, or he smells like it. Drunk and sick. Sunni Chutney is going to go nuts."

It was an understatement.

For the second time in two days she called dispatch for help. This time she told them she had a young male who appeared to be in an alcoholic stupor. She didn't mention any names. The last thing she needed was rumors about Billy spreading all over the county, even before the mayor found out.

By the time the paramedics arrived, she had managed to turn Billy onto his side and had just avoided him throwing up on her. She couldn't awaken him, and his breathing sounded bad. His skin felt clammy and was terribly pale. A deep cut on his forehead had bled a lot. Her probing fingers had also discovered another ugly cut just above his ear.

She also took time to take a few pictures with her cell phone. Eventually she was going to have to get a camera.

She never had any doubt who he was but there was a wallet in his back pocket with his college identification, a driver's license, and a five-dollar bill. He had keys in another pocket and thirty-five cents in change. She put it all in a zip-log bag she borrowed from Cal's kitchen. She also borrowed a piece of tape and wrote the date down on it.

Jodi walked with the paramedics out to the ambulance. She watched it pull out of the parking area as she rang Dr. Theo. It rang several times before it was answered.

"Did you call to complain about the size of your new place?" Dr. Theo said.

"On the contrary. It's perfect for me. And reasonable. No, I'm calling about something else."

Dr. Theo immediately sensed the tension in her words. "What?"

"I just found Billy Chutney in the back of Blackbeard's Tavern. I'm having him transported to County hospital. He's unconscious and he reeks of alcohol. His pulse is fast, his skin clammy. There's a nasty cut on his head. I'm no doctor but it looks bad. I thought you might want to be at the hospital."

"Of course," Dr. Theo said. "I'm there already, in fact. Are you coming?"

"Yes. Shortly. I want to look around here a little more. Somebody should notify the mayor and I have no idea where he is."

"I'll take care of that," Dr. Theo said. "I'll have Eunice call."

"Lots of luck with that," Jodi said.

Dr. Theo laughed and rang off.

She kept her cell phone in her hand and walked back around the back. She took pictures of the broken window and then went inside to take more pictures of the freezer and the mess in the main dining area. She knew sooner or later she was going to have to get around to writing reports on finding the dead woman and on finding Billy. She would almost certainly spend some time in court, and she wanted to get everything written down as she remembered it.

She was pretty sure Billy had not been alone in Blackbeard's Tavern. It would have taken more than one person to cause all that damage. And there were no cars around. Billy must have arrived in an automobile, so where was it now?

She looked around the back door and found nothing except mud. She followed the narrow trail down to the water's edge. There had never been a beach here, only a short drop-off into the water. It was protected by a metal fence. Nobody had ever been seriously injured but a few drunks had broken bones.

The water was up a lot higher.

She started to turn away and her eyes noticed something out of place. She bent. A single pearl was sitting on top of the mud. She had a sudden sickening feeling the pearl would match all the others on the shoe the dead woman was wearing.

She put it in the bag even though she had a bad feeling she was about to stir up a hornet's nest.

If the pearl matched, there was a good chance the dead woman had been in Blackbeard's Tavern. With the mayor's son.

It would not be that much of a struggle to drag something from the back of the tavern to the drop-off. And the tides would be right to move something down the beach to the area where Freddie Thigpen had found the woman.

17.

She intended to follow the ambulance to the hospital but changed her mind and stopped off at the courthouse. She wanted to make sure Eunice got the message. She nearly changed her mind again as she stepped in the doorway of Eunice's office.

Eunice sat stiffly at her desk, her face pale. Loose scraps of gray hair framed her face, and her cheeks were wet with tears. She held a pencil and she was violently drawing black circles on her desktop calendar. Jodi started backing away, but she was not quick enough. Eunice looked up. It took a moment for her eyes to focus, and something like a soft sob tore form the back of her throat.

"It can't be true," Eunice said.

"What can't be true?" Jodi asked.

"About Billy?"

"It's true. Have you contacted the mayor?"

"Dr. Theo called me. I said I couldn't do it. She took the mayor's number. She'll call."

Jodi nodded. Eunice was clearly incapable of doing it.

"And somebody from the hospital called. A nurse. She wanted to talk to the mayor, and when I told her he wasn't available, she said I needed to find him and tell him that his son was in the hospital badly hurt." Eunice made a sobbing sound. "The nurse said he'd been drinking," Eunice said. "I don't believe it. He's always been a good boy. So polite. He's not like some of the other little hoodlums in town."

The mayor had not mentioned any hoodlums in his pep talk. He kept stressing the lack of crime in the city. She was beginning to understand why they called him Slick.

"Is he going to be okay?" Eunice asked.

It occurred to Jodi that Eunice's deep feeling for Billy seemed a little more than just sympathy for the boss's son.

"I don't know. Dr. Theo is with him and you know she's a good doctor. I'm sure they're doing everything they can." She took a few steps closer to Eunice and put hand comfortingly on her shoulder. "Are you good friends with Billy."

"Me?" Eunice grew flustered. "No. Of course not. He comes in sometime. He seems nice."

Jodi figured she still had plenty of time if the mayor was coming from Atlanta. All she could do in the hospital was sit around in the waiting room. She still couldn't get into her office and she was hungry again. She knew the sandwich shop by the hospital had fantastic chocolate doughnuts and good coffee. Better than waiting in a cold, sterile waiting room, and she knew Dr. Theo would call if there was any news.

She got a phone call as soon as she drove out of the police station parking lot. She didn't recognize the number, but she recognized Frances' high-pitched voice.

"The locksmith will be there to meet us first thing in the morning," Frances said.

"Great," Jodi said.

"I've also been thinking about money."

"Oh?"

"Your top staff person in administration makes the same thing as a watch Lieutenant, and that's nearly as much as I made as the mayor's secretary."

"That sounds fair to me," Jodi said. "Of course, I don't even know for sure what I'm making."

"We'll figure it out together," Frances said. "This is really going to make Sunni happy."

"Sunni's got other stuff to worry about right now," Jodi said.

They had Billy in the emergency room when Jodi reached the hospital. She found a seat in one of the uncomfortable chairs in the waiting room along with a half-dozen other people. A small television mounted one wall was showing the weather. The drizzling rain showed no signs of tapering off. There was another storm forming.

Hopefully, it would not come Sandy Shoals way.

Dr. Theo came through the doors into the waiting room.

"Don't get up," she said, settling into the chair next to me.

"You look like you've had a busy day," Jodi said.

"I'm going to have to retire from my retirement," Dr. Theo said.

"How is Billy?" Jodi asked.

Dr. Theo paused before answering, and Jodi knew she was thinking about how much she could say.

"I'm glad you found him when you did. I don't know how long he's been out of it, but probably a good while. He has a serious concussion. We also had his stomach pumped.

"Life threatening?" Jodi asked.

“Possibly,” Dr. Theo admitted. “Time will tell. You did the smart thing calling me. Slick and I don't always get along, but he trusts me as a doctor. And I see no reason for this to be fodder for the gossip mill. Hopefully, we can keep this on the QT."

"It may be too late for that," Jodi said.

"I don't understand," Dr. Theo said.

"There's something else, something I don't even like thinking about."

"What?" Dr. Theo said, alarm in her voice.

"First, tell me if Billy had any scratches on him. If there are, we need to get photographs of them."

"Scratches? What kind of scratches?" Dr. Theo's eyes widened in understanding. "You're thinking of the woman you found on the beach? You don't even know if it was a drowning until the coroner does his autopsy, but you suspect Billy. Billy couldn't do anything like that. I brought him into the world."

"I'm sure you're right," Jodi said.

"Not Billy," Dr. Theo insisted.

Dr. Theo said nothing else for a few moments and then she got up and left the room. The minutes went by painfully slow, like the last few minutes of an algebra class. When Dr. Theo returned, she looked relieved.

"No scratches of any kind," she said.

Relief was short-lived because a moment later they were interrupted by the arrival of Mayor Chutney and his entourage. They must have been a lot closer than Atlanta. A tall, immaculately groomed young man in a Sandy Shoals police uniform led the way into the room, bristling with self-importance. Jodi felt an instant dislike for the muscular, handsome young policeman.

Sunni Chutney was the last to enter the room, but she swept by everyone. She ignored Jodi and came to a shuddering halt in front of Dr. Theo.

Kate had once described Sunni as trailer park trash promoted to royalty.

It was a cruel but apt description. Almost as tall as Jodi, but much more voluptuous. Her hair thick and blond, her eyes green. She wore lots of makeup and tottered on six-inch heels. Jodi had always wondered how she had managed to get her eyebrows the same color of her obviously dyed hair, but never had the courage to ask.

She was worshiped by her husband, and she terrified everyone else.

"Where is he?" Sunni demanded. "I want to see him now. That silly little girl at the front desk wouldn't tell me anything."

One person in town who wasn't intimidated by Sunni was Dr. Theo.

"Perhaps we should go somewhere private and talk about this," Dr. Theo suggested.

Slick picked up on the warning note in Dr. Theo's voice and he grabbed his wife by the arm.

"Yes, honey. Let's find a quiet room."

Sunni savagely shook off his hand.

"I want to know what's wrong with my son," she demanded, loud enough for everyone in the waiting room to look up with interest.

"He was struck on the head," Dr. Theo said. "It's possible he's also suffering from alcohol poisoning."

"Impossible," Sunni said, her voice loud again. "None of my children touch alcohol."

Sunni balled up her fists. For a moment Jodi thought she was going to attack Dr. Theo, but then she started shaking and grew pale. Jodi recognized the signs of shock and she was out of her seat immediately, one arm around Sunni to keep her from collapsing on the floor.

Slick put his arm around her other side and between them they maneuvered her over to a chair and helped her sit. Jodi had an uncharitable thought that Sunni resembled a plastic inflatable doll that had been somehow punctured, and all the air was slowly leaking out.

"I don't understand," Sunni said. "How could this happen?"

There was no answer anybody could make to that.

Nobody tried.

18.

Jodi felt an ugly mood coming on and she decided to introduce herself to her officer. It was probably the wrong time for introductions. Everything about him, from his military crispness, his short, styled hair, his smug sense of arrogance, irritated her.

She was going to have to sit him down and have a long conversation about his responsibilities, but for now she just wanted to vent, and he was available.

"I'm your new chief," she said.

He nodded, without speaking.

"Has it occurred to you for the past three days that your presence was needed in the city of Sandy Shoals?"

"Uncle Roland needed me," he said.

“Your Uncle Roland needed you,” Jodi repeated his words in exasperation. Then she counted to ten slowly in her head. “Well, he doesn’t need you right now, and our city does. And the city pays your salary. So, what I’d like for you to do right now is get into your patrol car, check in with the dispatcher in the sheriff’s office, and answer a few calls. You know, police work. The kind of stuff you were hired to do.”

He glared at her. She could tell he felt the same about her as she felt about him, but at least she had broken through his smug exterior. He glanced at his uncle for support, but his uncle was busy with Sunni. Jodi knew he still might refuse and if he did, she might as well turn in her keys and head back to Athens. She couldn't run a department if there was even one officer who wouldn't respect her position.

“I'm driving the limousine," he protested.

"Then take the limousine back to the police impound yard and change it for a patrol car," she said sweetly. "And we are going to have to sit down together soon. And discuss your responsibilities with the department."

He glanced at the mayor again, but Slick still wasn't paying any attention. Or perhaps he was because Jodi had seen him looking out of the corner of his eyes, and she was sure he had heard everything being said. But he didn't interfere, and his nephew finally took the keys from Jodi's hand and stalked out of the waiting room.

Jodi breathed a sigh of relief.

There was not much else she could do until Billy Chutney woke up, if he woke up. She made her way back out to her car and sat listening to her officer receive an accident call from county dispatch. The rain was coming harder. It was beginning to depress her. She was started to feel waterlogged. She preferred her water underneath a boat.

She started to check back and glanced over to see two men standing underneath the hospital awning at the emergency entrance. One of them was unmistakably Geoff Hamilton. Even from a distance, there was just something about him she found charismatic.

The other man was a little shorter than Geoff and had bright red hair. His name was Robert Weathers. People in the community called him Bud.

She called him Dad.

She debated not getting out, but she was curious as to what her father was doing at the hospital. And talking to Geoff. She was also aware that she was going to keep running into him around town and Dr. Theo was right about her not being able to avoid both him and Kate for very long.

She made up her mind and got out of her car and walked over to them. Her father didn't try to hug her. Her father's comforting hugs had been an important part of her childhood years, but he had learned they were no longer welcome. Things were still tense between them.

She might have hugged Geoff, but he didn't offer.

"What are you doing here?" she asked her father.

He looked hesitant.

"Is it Kate?" she asked.

She hated the sound of concern in her voice. Her dad must have noticed it, but he pretended he didn't. The hurtful emotions were still too close the surface.

"Kate's fine," he said "She'd rather be back at the marina helping to clean things up, but she had an appointment with Dr. Theo, and I made her come."

She noticed the hesitancy in his words. He was lying about something. He was never a good liar. She wondered if there was something going on with Kate that was more serious. She felt tempted to ask, but she didn't want to seem overly concerned. Instead, she turned to Geoff.

"I just met the city's only working officer," Jodi said. "I think I want to fire him."

"That didn't take long," Geoff said. "But firing Hollis will probably be more trouble than it's worth. It would put you in bad with Sunni."

"I may already be in trouble with Sunni," Jodi said. "I hired Frances San."

Geoff laughed. "You don't mess around."

"Now all I need is to hire a bunch of other deputies."

The thought was depressing. Jodi remembered how long it took her to get hired with the campus police. There was an application and a background check, testing, and then six weeks of training.

“I have a suggestion for you,” Geoff said. “You might want to find officers who are already certified by the state of Georgia.”

“And how would I do that?”

“Frances can help. Put some ads in the paper. You might get some officers who already work for other places. Possibly even a few of the county deputies might want to join.”

“You mean steal them?” Jodi asked.

“That’s such a crass way of putting it,” Geoff said. “And I do know a few guys who aren’t all that happy with the current sheriff.”

Her dad's cell phone rang he answered it. "Kate's ready. I'm going to go fetch her." He looked at Jodi inquiringly. "You want to come along?"

Jodi shook her head. "I don't think so."

Her father looked a little hurt as he put his cell phone back into his pocket and went through the emergency doors into the hospital. She caught Geoff's look and she wasn't sure she liked it.

"What?" she asked.

He shrugged. "None of my business."

"That's right," she said.

19.

She parked in the street. Frances San was waiting for her on the front steps of the police department.

There was no longer a lock on the front door of the police department, just a gaping hole.

The locksmith had finally arrived. A small, dark and nervous man named Adamo.

"I will replace this with a regular lock, and give you the key," he said. "I've already reset the code on the back door lock. Right now, it's just a sequence of six fours. You can change it to a number you prefer."

"Thank you," Jodi said.

Just inside the front door was a spacious reception area A counter took up most of the room. There were two doors on each side of the reception area, and they found that both were locked.

"Wait," Frances said.

She went behind the from counter and pressed a button under the top. The electronic lock of the door disengaged, and Jodi opened it to reveal a long, musty smelling hallway. On the left side of the hall there were three doors. All of them were small offices with desktop computers. Paperwork was scattered messily on all the desks. She took a quick glance at a file folder and saw it was an arrest report.

"It's worse than I thought," Frances said. "Sensitive information left lying around. A lawsuit in the making. Something else the sheriff would love to know about."

The other side of the hallway had two doors, and both were locked.

"I think that's the interview room," Frances said. "The other is an evidence room."

They made the rest of the tour through the department. Someone had left a pile of dirty uniforms in the middle of the hallway. Another pile a little farther on. It seemed like every fired officer had left a pile of uniforms and equipment in the floor.

“Classy,” Jodi said.

There were larger offices in the back and several supply rooms, all of them locked. The largest office was in the back corner and had a window looking out at the parking lot. It was furnished with an old, scarred wooden desk that looked as if it had once been a teacher's desk, a swivel office chair that didn't swivel because a roller was broken, and a straight-back chair that looked as if it might be possibly be made of cheap plywood.

The entire room smelled of stale cigarette smoke.

"Chief Ballard's office," Frances said.

"I figured."

The office had a closet that was empty and a private bathroom with a shower. The shower looked as if it had not been thoroughly cleaned in a long time the cabinet by the sink was piled high with magazines, all of them featuring scantily clad women. The odor of cigarette smoke was even stronger, almost suffocating.

There was also a half-filled bottle of scotch.

"It looks as if Chief Ballard preferred single malt."

Her cell phone rang.

"I thought you might want to know," Dr. Theo said. "You were right. It's definite the woman on the beach was strangled, but so far, she can't be identified. Her fingerprints aren’t showing up in any of the data bases. Evidently she's never been arrested."

"Or applied for any security jobs," Jodi said.

"Exactly. They're going to put her vital statistics and a description of her tattoos out on their computer. Hopefully, somebody will recognize her."

She clicked off. Jodi thought of the familiar looking tattoo again and wondered if it was worth a trip to Athens to talk to Cat Esterhazy. Earlier she had thought to share the information with Detective Blankenship, but now she wasn't sure. She had no confidence in his investigative skills, and the tiny pearl kept bothering her. It probably did come from the dead woman's shoe, and it meant she was at Blackbeard's Tavern.

Could it have been during the storm, and was Billy Chutney there at the same time?

Could the mayor's son be involved in her death?

She put her cell phone away and followed Frances through the rest of the department. In the rear they found an evidence room, wide open. The lock was busted. Strewn along the shelves were dozens of tagged boxes, some of them containing weapons used in crimes, some of them supposedly containing drugs. Jodi was afraid to look.

If evidence was missing?

"This is a mess," Jodi said.

"A big fire would help," Frances said.

"Don't even joke about that," Jodi said. "I think we're cursed."

Jodi needed a moment to think. She stopped in her office and sat down in the chair behind the desk. It was terribly uncomfortable. If it had conformed to Bob Ballard's body through the years, then Chief Ballard must have had some strange lumps in places. She wiggled around a little. It didn't help.

She had a slight headache. She tried to force herself to relax by thinking of the Gypsy. It had been so long since she had been out on her boat, feeling the waves under the bow, smelling the sea air.

The smell of sea air was suddenly very strong. She opened her eyes. In the chair opposite, the one she feared was nothing, but a few scraps of plywood glued together, a dead woman sat.

"Oh, no, no, no no," she said.

It was the woman from the beach still wearing her tattered outfit and one white shoe, but fortunately with her long hair covering the side of her face where the crabs had been busy.

The strong scent of ocean and seafood became almost suffocating in the room. It was a smell Jodi had always loved.

Now it made her feel a little nauseated.

Jodi had convinced herself she wasn't crazy. In fact, she repeated it to herself sometimes as sort of a personal mantra. There was some logical reason she saw Timothy, a weird shorting of the synapses in her brain. She was learning to deal with it, and eventually she was sure she would no longer see him.

But seeing the dead woman in her new office was one ghost too many.

"Where am I?" the woman asked. "Who are you?"

"My name is Jodi Weathers," Jodi said. "You're currently in the Sandy Shoals police station."

"Why? Have I been arrested?"

"Not quite," Jodi said.

The woman looked puzzled, and Jodi was not surprised. She could hold a conversation with Timothy, but her dead ex-husband could never answer a direct question. It always made him frown just like the woman was frowning.

If she had to see ghosts, why couldn't they at least help her out, give her information?

"I don't feel well," the woman said.

"I'm not sure you can feel anything," Jodi said. "I mean, I hate to be the one to tell you, but you're dead."

The woman looked alarmed. "I don't want to be dead."

"I don't think there's anything either of us can do about it," Jodi said.

"How did I die?" the woman asked.

Jodi shook her head.

"Did somebody kill me?" she asked.

Jodi sat up as straight as she could in the sagging desk chair. Now this was interesting.

"Why would somebody want to kill you?" she asked.

The woman looked confused again. It seemed to be just as frustrating for her as it was for Jodi.

"It's not fair," the woman said again

Timothy always seemed to just vanish when he left her, but this woman seemed to fade away. She grew more transparent with the passing seconds and then disappeared completely in a kind of vapor. Jodi figured her psychosis was getting more imaginative.

She checked the chair before she left.

Of course, it wasn't wet. Ninny.

20.

The rain was still coming down softly when Jodi left the duplex the next morning. The afternoon before she had gone shopping and practically cleaned out what was left of her meager bank account. But she thought her new tennis shoes and blue sweats looked nice. She crossed the street and entered Veteran's Park. In the wet grass she did a few stretches and then started a slow jog on one of the narrow trails. An hour later she came running out of the park to find Geoff sitting on the porch swing with two mugs of coffee.

"I saw you coming up the trail," he said. "I thought you might want this."

"You got up so early just to make me coffee?" she said.

"I have an ulterior purpose," he said.

"Good coffee can get you almost anywhere with me," she said.

"I also make an excellent ham and cheese omelet," he said. “The trick is to add just the right amount of mushrooms and bell peppers to give it a distinct flavor.”

"I'd love to have you make me breakfast sometime," she said, and then blushed at the implication of her words.

"But I can't today," she said quickly. “I have an appointment with someone named Louis Sutter. He says he must talk to me about finances. He sounded urgent.”

“Louis is the city's comptroller,” Geoff said. “He's a financial guru, but he does upset easily. He probably wants to talk about the city budget.”

Jodi shook her head in despair.

"Take Frances with you," Geoff suggested. "If anyone knows more about city finances than Louis, it's Frances."

"Anything to help me with the numbers," Jodi said. She settled back in the swing. "But you're not bringing me coffee just to talk about my appointments. What's got you up so early?"

Geoff sat down in the porch swing and she sat beside him. Their legs touched. It was kind of nice even if it was by accident.

"Billy Chutney," Geoff said.

"Is his condition worse?" Jodi asked, in alarm.

"No different," Geoff said. "But Aunt Theo called me before daylight this morning. Detective Blankenship has been around asking questions about Billy."

"I was afraid of that," Jodi said. "Billy and the woman at the beach were possibly at Blackbeard's Tavern at the same time. Even the ineptest detective would eventually make a connection, especially now that we know the woman was strangled. I am surprised that Blankenship got onto it so fast."

"He wanted to talk to Aunt Theo, but she wasn't there. He talked to the ward nurse. He wanted her to wake Billy up so he could talk to him. He got kind of nasty about it before she finally convinced him that Billy was in a coma, and nobody could wake him up. Yet."

"Why did Aunt Theo call you?" Jodi asked. "How are you involved?"

"Aunt Theo seems to think Billy is need of a lawyer," Geoff said.

It took a moment for the implication of Geoff's words to settle in. She did a mental backflip. "Wait. You're a lawyer?"

Geoff looked a little sheepish. "Both my dad and Grandfather Gus were unhappy with the idea that I wanted to spend my life doing carpentry work. They insisted I go to college, and

Theo and my mother sided with them. They forged a bond I couldn't break. They insisted on either law or medicine. Medicine required a lot longer in school, so I chose law."

"Seriously," Jodi said.

"Not by choice, but by necessity," he said. "I wimped out to my family. But I admit it comes in handy sometimes. I help friends out of trouble when I can."

"And Theo wants you to help Billy," Jodi said.

Geoff shrugged. "He might not need it. He hasn't been charged with anything."

"Wouldn't his parents be the ones to choose a lawyer?" Jodi asked.

"They're kind of out of it right now," Geoff said. "But I'm meeting with them in an hour at the hospital. And they'll probably take Aunt Theo's advice. Pretty much everyone in Sandy Shoals does."

"Are you any good at criminal law?" she asked.

"Why?"

"Because I'm afraid it's going to take someone really good."

"You think he's guilty," Geoff said perceptively.

"I think it's a possibility," she said.

She drove out to Hwy 17 and went through a drive-through for more coffee and a breakfast burrito. She passed her officer on the way. She had been listening on the radio and the county had given him an accident call. He stood with his clipboard at the side of the road. He wore a yellow rain slicker. He glared at her as she drove past. He didn't look happy.

Some things made life better.

She parked her car in the police parking lot, and saw Frances getting out of a red Volvo. Frances wore a skirt, blouse, and heels. Her hair was in a bun. Her make-up carefully applied. She looked totally competent, totally professional. It made Jodi feel a little dowdy.

"You've got sauce on your chin," Frances said.

Jodi wiped her chin with a napkin. "I have a meeting with our finance person this morning. I would appreciate it if you would come with me. This guy sounded a little strange over the phone."

Frances laughed. "Louis is strange. Nice, but strange. He's our finance person and our city attorney. I think he got his legal degree from a mail order catalogue, but he's competent enough. I think you'll find meeting him an experience."

"I'd still like you along, to help with the financial stuff."

"Sure," Frances said.

Jodi wasn't sure she wanted anymore experiences. The meeting was in the mayor's conference room, just next door to his office. Eunice gave her a friendly nod as she passed, but her eyes widened in alarm as she saw Frances. A man stood waiting in the conference room. For a moment, Jodi thought she had stepped back in time.

The man wore a suit that looked as if it belonged to the thirties. He wore a suit that was a funny color green, a white shirt with a stiff collar, and a red bowtie. His shoes were highly polished. His eyes also widened in surprise but not alarm as he saw Frances. He had thick dark hair, carefully combed, and he was average height. He wore heavy glasses.

"I didn't expect you, Frances," he said.

"Am I not welcome?" Frances asked.

"Of course," he said. "It's good to see you. Would you ladies like coffee? I've got it ready."

"I have some," Jodi said, holding up her cup.

"I'd like some, Louis," Frances said.

Evidently Louis already knew how Frances liked her coffee because he poured her a cup and added sugar before he brought it to her. There was something more than admiration as he looked at Frances.

"You have a fan," Jodi said, as he moved back to the head of the wide conference table.

"We're friends," Frances said.

"Friends," Jodi said. "It looked like he was going to bow kneel at your feet.”

"He just has courtly manners," Frances insisted.

"It goes along with his bowtie," Jodi said.

Louis cleared his throat. "I'm afraid we might have a problem with the police department."

"You mean, other than there being only one officer and the doors being locked?" Jodi asked.

"Yes. Another issue."

"Out with it, Louis," Frances insisted.

"Sandy Shoals pays for the first initial issue of five sets of uniforms. The cost is then taken out of the officer's paycheck until it is paid off. The officer is also issued all equipment needed. If the officer then quits, or gets fired, a hold is put on his final paycheck until it's determined his uniforms have been paid off and all equipment has been turned back in."

"We know all that, Louis," Frances said. "Chief Ballard was responsible for making sure everything was done correctly."

"Yes," Louis said, "but Chief Ballard left the job unexpectedly."

"He was fired," Frances said.

"Yes, well, the issue is that in Chief Ballard's absence, it fell to his second in command to take care of these details."

"Who was also fired," Frances pointed out.

"Yes," Louis said. "It all eventually fell back on the mayor's office to make sure everything was done properly. That would have been you, Frances, but you were no longer here."

Francs shrugged. "At least I wasn't fired. But I think I know where this is going. Nobody put a hold on the officer's paychecks and a lot of their equipment walked out the door with them."

"Unfortunately," Louis said. "Well, everything except their weapons. We did get all the weapons back. The sheriff's department handled that part of it. But all of the uniforms and equipment will be charged back to the police budget."

"Some of it was left in the hallways," Jodi said.

"It will still be a considerable cost," he said.

The meeting wasn't finished with the bad news. Jodi had to suffer through two more hours of financial detail. Sutter said it was things she needed to know as chief. Jodi hoped Frances was listening and understanding. Sutter showed chart after chart of manpower statistics, salaries, insurance, and benefits until the numbers were all jumbled together in Jodi's mind.

"I am still of the opinion we could use the money we spend for a police department more wisely in other areas," he said. "The sheriff's department is capable of handling the police routine."

"Everyone knows that's your opinion," Frances said.

"I take it he's not a big fan of the city police," Jodi said as they walked back to the station.

"He's such a sweet man," Frances said, "but he doesn't understand anything but numbers. It makes no financial sense to him to have both a sheriff's department and a city police department with the same kind of functions. When the police scandal hit, he thought it was the perfect time to do away with the city police. He nearly got his head handed to him and he still can't understand why. It really hurt his feelings."

"Would it not make sense for the sheriff's department to take everything over," Jodi said. "It's a duplication of effort. Especially with the administrative part."

"Don't go there," Frances warned. "It's a political quagmire. Both the Sheriff and the Mayor are elected politicians. They both answer to the people who voted them in office. The locals would prefer their own department answerable only to them, instead of a sheriff's department answerable to the entire county. And even the argument Louis made about lower taxes is a farce. The taxes wouldn't be lowered. The city would use the money for something else. Politicians never give money back. And it would put us both out of work."

"There is that," Jodi admitted.

"And I don't like the sheriff," Frances said. "I'm not saying he's a crook or incompetent. He's just a blustery man who likes having his own way. And he has a lot in common with Bob Ballard."

“How so?”

“He’s smarter than Bob ever was. He stays politically correct. But you’ll quickly see he has the minimum number of minorities and women on the force. And he prefers the women in secretarial jobs, rather than on the street. “

“Oh, it really sounds like we’re going to get along,” Jodi said.

Frances laughed.

Her cell phone rang. Geoff.

"I thought you might want to know. Blankenship is on his way out to Blackbeard's Tavern with a crime scene van."

"They're moving fast," Jodi said.

“The Chutneys want me as Billy’s lawyer for the time being,” he said. “And Theo suggests you might want to go out to the Tavern yourself, just to watch over things. Right now, you, me, and his parents are the only ones who believe Billy is innocent."

"I'm not so sure about me," Jodi said.

21.

The slow, penetrating rain hadn't stopped, but it seemed to be coming from a different direction.

Wonderful.

A crime scene van, a black unmarked Ford with police antenna and a Sandy Shoals police car were parked in front of Blackbeard's Tavern. Seeing the Sandy Shoals police car made her take a deep breath and count to ten. Counting was advice given to her by her father the first time she had come home with a black eye and a note from her teacher.

"I know you come by it naturally with your red hair," he had told her, "but your temper is going to get you into trouble one day."

She should have counted to ten a half dozen times before she married Timothy.

She spotted her officer coming around the corner of the building. She had never seen anybody who fit the written description of sauntering, but her officer sauntered. He had his fingers hooked on his belt and he looked filled with self-importance. She counted to ten again, but it did no good. She was going to burst his bubble.

He came closer and had to jump back as she slammed her car door opened and took three steps to tower above him. He might have been very male and very muscular, but she had long ago learned how to use her height to intimidate when she needed to.

"What are you doing?" he asked. His voice came out a squeak.

"The better question is, what are you doing?" she asked. "There was a call a moment ago. A theft by taking at one of the stores along the boulevard. A county officer had to handle it because you were busy. Busy doing what?"

"The sheriff's department asked for my help," he said defensively.

"And you didn't check first with me?" she asked.

"I didn't have to check with Chief Ballard every time I did something," he said.

Something in his voice told her that what he really meant was that he didn't like taking orders from her. She wondered if it was her personally he didn't like, or just taking orders from a woman.

She counted to ten again. "Times have changed. If you're not on the street answering calls, I want to know where you are and what you are doing."

"That's treating me like a child," he said.

"You do what I tell you, or you quit. Those are your choices."

"The Sheriff's department would give me a job in a heartbeat," he said.

"Then what are you waiting on?" Jodi asked.

He wanted so badly to quit, but somehow controlled himself.

"Well, if you're not quitting at the moment," Jodi said. "Then tell me what Blankenship wanted from you."

"Just looking around the building," he said.

"Searching for anything in particular?" she asked.

Hollis shrugged. "He had us looking for a shoe."

She nodded. She was pretty sure she knew what shoe Blankenship was looking for, and if he found it here, he could certainly put the woman inside Blackbeard's Tavern. Of course, he could already do it if she told him about the pearl. The thought gave her a little twinge of guilt.

"You go back to work," she told Hollis. "Now. And remember in the future that you work for me and not the sheriff's department."

"Perhaps not for long," he said.

He said it as if it were a threat.

"You may be right about that," she said pleasantly. "Especially when your uncle finds out you were working with Detective Blankenship to find evidence to put his son in jail."

Jodi doubted he understood what was going on until that moment. His shoulders slumped. He walked over and climbed slowly into his car. He didn't look at Jodi as he drove away.

Jodi went in search of Blankenship and found him in the back of the building talking a crime scene guy. She heard part of the conversation before Blankenship noticed her. The crime scene guy was saying something about too many fingerprints before Blankenship stopped him with a raised hand.

"We need to talk," Jodi said.

The often-walked path behind the Tavern was still slick. With the rain falling so steady, it was going to take a while for it to dry out. She led Blankenship out to the drop-off to the beach.

"It wouldn't have taken somebody very strong to drag her out here," he said.

"And you've already made up your mind," Jodi said. "You sure tend to jump to conclusions, don't you? First, you didn't think it was murder. Now that it's murder, you automatically assume the mayor's kid is guilty."

"Something happened here," Blankenship said. "He was found drunk. He didn't break in by himself. Maybe the woman broke in with him. The sheriff thinks..."

Blankenship stopped talking, turned slightly pale. She realized he had revealed too much by mentioning the Sheriff.

"What does the sheriff think?" Jodi asked. "Perhaps that it would be a good thing politically for him if Billy Chutney was accused of murder. It might even change some people's minds about letting the county take over the police work on a permanent basis. At the very least, it would be embarrassing for the mayor."

"We just want to solve a murder," Blankenship protested.

"Sure," Jodi said. "But let's have a few ground rules. From now on, you'll let me know what's going on. No more secrets."

"Can't do that," he said. "You'd go straight to the mayor."

"Here's the thing," Jodi said. "There's politics on both sides. You and I both know what's going on. If I can't get you to corporate with me, then I'm going to ask the GBI to step in and take over the investigation."

"The sheriff wouldn't like that," Blankenship said.

"He won't like if I go to the news people and talk about his political agenda either," Jodi threatened. "And something else you might consider while you're searching for clues around here?"

"What?" he asked.

"If Billy and the woman were together, how did they get here? Where's their car?"

"The storm," he said.

"The surge didn't come up this far," she said.

They might have continued the conversation a little longer except Jodi noticed Bianca walking toward them. She wore one of her outlandish colorful outfits, but it was what she had on her feet that immediately drew Jodi's attention. She had an unlaced tennis shoe on one foot. On her other foot she wore a white heel with lots of straps. And pearls.

A Jimmy Choo.

22.

She dreaded what was going to come next.

Howard Blankenship was ecstatic. The shoe was real evidence the dead woman had been in the area of Blackbeard's Tavern, and now all that was left was to prove Billy and the dead woman had some sort of relationship. Howard was already talking about traveling to Athens, searching Billy's apartment, talking to his friends.

Jodi hoped no relationship could be proved, but she had a bad feeling it was a futile hope.

It still didn't prove Billy killed her, but a good district attorney could already put a scenario together. Billy was drunk. Enamored of an older woman. The woman wanted to break it off, or something along those lines. There was a fight during the storm. Billy strangled her and then carried her out to the drop-off and dumped her in the ocean. But then how was Billy injured? Flying debris? Something struck him and he dragged himself back into the tavern before he passed out.

The case was weak, but it could be made to fit the circumstances.

Especially if evidence kept piling up.

She checked back in and was immediately informed by the county dispatch that it was urgent she return to the Sandy Shoals station house.

She smelled the sea almost as soon as she pulled out away from the tavern.

"Is this where I died?" the woman said.

"I think so," Jodi said.

"I don't like being dead," she said.

"I'm sorry," Jodi said.

Jodi wanted to kick herself for apologizing to a ghost. A ghost who probably wasn't there.

But since she was.

"I'm really tired of calling you the dead woman," Jodi said. "Don't you have a name?"

The woman looked at her in confusion. Light shone through her so that she seemed to shimmer, and then she disappeared.

"A lot of help you are," Jodi said.

The lock on the front door had been replaced and Frances San was waiting inside in the reception area.

"Freddie Thigpen," Frances said.

"What about him?"

"He's here to confess," Frances said.

"To what?" Jodi asked.

"The Brinks robbery. The Lindbergh kidnapping. You take your choice. Anything and everything. But he also claims he knows something about the dead woman on the beach."

Jodi shook her head. "Unbelievable."

"Even if I hated this job, I couldn't quit now," Frances said. "It's like a soap opera. I have to find out what happens next."

"I'm glad somebody is enjoying it," Jodi said. "Where is he?"

"He's in the largest interview room. I got him a soda. But we have another problem. I know Chief Ballard had video cameras installed in the interview rooms because I saw the bills, and there's a cabinet in the evidence room that's full of videos. But if you want to tape Freddie's confession, we'll have to run up to Best Buy. Someone sabotaged the cameras, at least that's what I suspect from all the bare wires hanging down."

"Great," Jodi said. "Can you take shorthand?"

"Perfectly," Frances said.

"Then I'll listen, and you write."

Frances had left the door open to the interview room, and there was good reason. Freddie still wore an abundance of clothing and his scent was nearly overpowering in the room. Jodi sat down at the table across from him. Frances had picked up a pad and pencil and she pulled a chair to the farthest corner of the room. Jodi couldn't blame her.

"You want to confess something, Freddie?" Jodi asked.

"I saw it," Freddie mumbled. "I saw the woman get killed."

Freddie wouldn't look up at her as he spoke. His shoulders slumped. He had his arms crossed over his chest. She had read in one of her psychology books that people who sat like that were trying to protect themselves.

She wondered what Freddie was protecting himself from.

She glanced at Frances and Frances shook her head sadly.

"All right, Freddie," Jodi said. "Tell me about it. Tell me what you saw."

He licked his lips. "It wasn't Billy."

"You saw someone, but it wasn't Billy. You're sure?"

"Yes. It was someone else. I didn't get a good look at him, but it wasn't Billy. A different man. Someone else."

"What were you doing there?"

He seemed confused by the question and shook his head as if to clear away mental cobwebs. "I was sleeping. She woke me up. Screaming."

"You were sleeping during a hurricane?" Jodi asked. "You slept when the water came up the beach all the way past the access road."

"No," he said. "You're confusing me. The storm came later. The water. That was later."

Jodi stood and Frances followed her back out into the hallway.

"Seriously," Jodi said, shaking her head.

“Sunni Chutney had a talk with Freddie,” Frances said. “I’m sure of it. I bet she offered him a few bottles of wine.”

“How would she have the time? Blankenship just started asking questions yesterday, and I doubt she understood that Billy was considered a suspect until she met with Geoff this morning.”

“Sunni is capable of almost anything,” Frances said. “If this doesn’t work, she might confess to murdering the woman herself.”

It was something that hadn't occurred to Jodi.

"And maybe her confession wouldn't be so far-fetched," Frances continued. "Sunni would not have been happy if she found out her precious son was going around with an older woman, especially if he was talking about making it a permanent relationship. I know she was supposed to be in Atlanta, but maybe she was following them somehow. She's a large, strong woman. She could have strangled someone."

"No," Jodi said. "I agree that she might be responsible for Freddie's confession, but she's not responsible for our dead woman. Not that I don't believe she could do it, but she would have never left Billy unconscious in the tavern. He nearly died."

"True," Frances said reluctantly.

"You really don't like her, do you," Jodi said.

"What gave you that idea?" Frances asked.

“I do think Billy is going to need a good lawyer before this is done," Jodi said.

"I understood he's got a good a lawyer already," Frances said.

"Geoffrey?" Jodi questioned. "He's a nice guy and I like him, but I think Billy's going to need someone with a lot of courtroom experience."

Frances laughed softly. "Geoff Hamilton was a Federal attorney for eight years in Washington. Then he was a partner in a Savannah law firm for a few years. He specialized in cases nobody else could win."

"He let me believe he only practiced law as a sideline," Jodi said. "What happened to him?"

"I think he just got burned out," Frances said. "He got tired of the fast pace."

Jodi nodded. Geoff was becoming more and more interesting.

She stepped back into the interview room. "Did someone tell you to say all this, Freddie?"

"Nobody," Freddie said, but his eyes grew evasive.

"Are you sure, Freddie?"

"It wasn't Billy," Freddie said obstinately.

"Okay, Freddie," Jodi said. "We've got your statement. Frances will have it typed up later, and you'll sign it."

Freddie put his hands-on top of the table, and he seemed to be staring at something far off. "He had a limp."

"What?"

"The man who dropped the girl off the cliff. He limped."

A limping man. Sunni must have coached Freddie in detail. Adding a limping man was something out of Sherlock Holmes.

Yet, it made her feel uneasy. It was an odd detail.

She walked Freddie back out to the front and watched as

he made his way down the steps. He turned off main street and started down Jolly Roger toward Baker. She wondered if he might have a shelter hidden away in some part of Veteran's Park. Eventually she was going to have to do something about Freddie, but she didn't know what.

He was one of society's lost ones.

There just seemed to be so many.

23.

Early the next morning Jodi went for a run in Veteran's Park. She needed to think. Running or going out on the Gypsy often cleared her mind. Helped her to focus.

She was sure Sunni had put Freddie up to the false confession, and it bothered her. Sunni could just be trying to get her son out of serious trouble, or it could be something else. Maybe Sunni knew Billy was guilty, or maybe, as Frances had suggested jokingly, Sunni was guilty herself.

If anyone could kill someone to protect her family, it was Sunni. Jodi could only imagine Sunni's temper tantrum when she found out that Billy was involved with an older woman.

The hurricane would seem tame in comparison.

But the limping man part kept tugging at her. Billy certainly didn't limp, and she knew of nobody else involved with the case. But somebody could have been hurt during the storm. It was hard for her to believe Sunni had coached Freddie well enough to come up with an idea for a mysterious limping man.

She thought more about the tattoo on the dead woman's back. Her police friend had suggested it was the work of an artist in Athens. It was a good possibility, and it would take a day to drive to Athens and talk to the artist. It was also a stretch. It was possibly not the same artist, and even if it was, the artist might not remember the customer.

But otherwise she was accomplishing exactly nothing.

Back at her apartment, she showered and dressed. Her cell phone beeped as she walked to the station.

The conversation was short. The mayor asked if she would meet him at the dough nut shop across from his Ford dealership on 17. He had already hung up before she could respond.

The lights were on and Frances was already at the station. At least by deciding to hire Frances, Jodi had accomplished one thing. The best decision she had made so far.

Practically her only decision.

Her own office was empty. Furniture gone. A tarp was on the floor and paint cans scattered about.

"I figured beige," Frances said, handing her a Styrofoam cup of coffee. "You can't go wrong with beige. I also have temps coming in this afternoon and we're going to start getting the files in order. On, and I have some employment forms for you to sign. They're in a folder at the reception desk. Do those and I can get you into the system to get paid. The swearing in ceremony will have to wait."

"You're the only one around here who knows what they are doing," Jodi said. "I'll sign the forms, and then I have to go see the mayor."

"Better you than me," Frances said.

Her cell phone rang as she climbed into her car.

The lowlife is at the hospital trying to wake up Billy again," Dr. Theo said. "This time he went in without asking the nurse. She found him shaking Billy."

"I don't have to ask what lowlife," Jodi said.

"The nurse ran him out of the room with a few choice words. I wish Gus was still alive. Gus would have had him horse whipped."

"I don't think you do that sort of thing anymore," Jodi said.

"The country would be better off if you could still horse whip a lowlife now and then."

"I'll talk to him," Jodi said.

"Oh, he doesn't like you either. He went after Slick and Sunni when he found out he wasn't going to be able to wake Billy up. He asked all sorts of questions. Nasty questions. He wanted to know what they knew about Billy's relationship with the dead woman. Sunni didn't handle it well. I've got her under sedation."

Jodi was tempted to tell Dr. Theo about Sunni's attempt to get Freddie to lie for her but decided against it.

"Maybe I should talk to the sheriff about him," Jodi said.

"Why? You don't think Blankenship is doing this on his own. He wouldn't have the nerve. The sheriff is behind everything he's doing."

"Maybe I can still get him to listen to reason," Jodi said.

"Somebody better," Dr. Theo said. "Or there's going to be another murder investigation. Only this time there's going to be no doubt who did it."

It was impossible to slam a cell phone down like an old-fashioned phone in a cradle, but somehow Dr. Theo gave the impression of doing it.

She drove slowly to a Duncan Donut across from the Chutney Ford dealership on 17. She wasn't looking forward to meeting with the Mayor, and she hoped Sunni wasn't with him.

Her stomach growled as she got out of her car and glanced at the front window where tantalizing doughnuts and chocolate eclairs were on display. She had planned on breakfast at the Smuggler's Café after a quick visit to check the progress at the station, but the Mayor's phone call followed by Dr. Theo's phone call had given her a sense of urgency.

The inside of the doughnut shop was warm and smelled sweet, and she was tempted to stop at the counter. A chocolate éclair was calling her name. She somehow walked past without stopping.

The Mayor was sitting by himself in the back, looking out the window at the rain. He had coffee and a plate of cream-filled doughnuts, but it didn't look like he was drinking or eating.

It was a very different Slick Chutney that had come to visit her in Athens. There was no trace of the smooth salesman. He sat slumped, and up close looked as if he was recovering from a three-day drunk. Unshaven, eyes bloodshot, hair uncombed, clothes that looked as if he had slept in them. He had a sour body odor, not as bad as Freddie, but still strong.

"Mayor Chutney," she said softly, and he looked up. His eyes didn't focus properly. He didn't seem to recognize her. "Slick?"

"I thought I'd have some doughnuts," he said, "but I don't want them."

"When is the last time you ate anything?" Jodi asked.

With her appetite, Jodi was always felt a strong sympathy for anyone going hungry.

"I don't know," he said. Something cleared up his eyes, and he finally seemed to know who she was. "Look, Jodi, I'm sorry about all this."

"About what?" Jodi asked.

"About this," he said. "All of this. I know this isn't what I promised when you were hired."

"It's okay, Mayor Chutney," she said. "Truth is, I suspected it wouldn't be all paperwork and public relations."

"I didn't expect a hurricane," he said. "And I didn't expect ... this... this thing."

Jodi patted the back of his hand. "I know it's upsetting. But we can't be sure of anything until Billy wakes up."

"What if he never wakes up," Mayor Chutney said.

"Dr. Theo is doing everything she can, and she's the best doctor I know. It'll be okay."

Jodi wasn't sure she believed what she was saying, but it wasn't the right place for harsh truth.

"And what happens if he does wake up," Mayor Chutney said, his voice trembling. "That awful policeman is making all sorts of threats. Sunni is already hysterical. She will die if he is arrested."

Jodi thought about taking one of his uneaten doughnuts. It probably said something about her character that she was thinking of food while the Mayor was suffering.

"Geoff will be there when he wakes up," Jodi said comfortingly. "I've been told Geoff is a very good lawyer."

Mayor Chutney nodded. Jodi looked at the doughnuts again, and then tried to take her mind off food.

"So, why did you want to see me?"

"That policeman came to see me. Blankenship. He wants my permission to search Billy's apartment in Athens. I refused. He says he'll get a warrant. Can he do that?"

"Yes," Jodi said.

"Then I want you to go there first. Today, if possible. I want you to get there before he does."

Jodi swallowed nervously. "Look, I'm not sure what you're asking of me, but if I searched his apartment, and found evidence, I'd have to share it with Blankenship. I couldn't hide it."

The fact she was already concealing information about the pearl she had found gave her another little twinge of guilt.

He shook his head. "I don't want you to hide anything. It's just that I know my son's not perfect. There maybe things there that I wouldn't want his mother to see. Things that might embarrass her. Like literature."

"Literature?" Jodi said. "You mean, like men's magazines."

He nodded. "Stuff like that."

"A lot of young college men probably have material like that lying around," Jodi said. "It's not the end of the world."

"It doesn't say much for their upbringing," Mayor Chutney said. "Sunni wouldn't like it. And anything that policeman finds, he'll tell everywhere. It'll be embarrassing."

Instinctively, Jodi knew the mayor was right about Blankenship.

"I'll give you written permission to search," Mayor Chutney said. "I'll give you the spare keys. But you must go today. Blankenship won't be wasting any time."

Jodi shook her head. "I'm still not sure it's a good idea. Judges can get kind of fussy about evidence tampering."

"I'm not asking you do that," Mayor Chutney said. "I'm just afraid there might be other things there. Private things. Things I wouldn't want that detective snickering about all over town."

Jodi still wasn't sure it was the right thing to do, but maybe searching Billy's apartment ahead of Blankenship might be a good idea. The detective seemed positive about Billy's guilt. Jodi couldn't hide evidence, but she also could make sure nothing was added. And she still wanted to talk to the tattoo person, however wasted a trip that might be.

"You're the mayor," Jodi said. "I guess that makes you my boss. I'll give Frances a call and let her know I'm on my way to Athens."

He nodded. He gave her written his permission already prepared and a handful of keys, one that opened Billy's apartment and the other for his car. She couldn't resist stopping at the counter for a large coffee and a couple of cream-filled doughnuts for the road.

She caught a last glimpse of the Mayor as she left the parking lot, still sitting hunched over, staring lifelessly out at the rain.

In a police car, her drive to Athens was a faster trip than she had made from Athens to Sandy Shoals. She rolled all the windows down on the trip and the stale cigarette smoke was a little less pungent when she reached Athens. It still wasn't completely gone. Maybe it would never be.

24.

The address for Billy's apartment was Hood Road, and she knew the area. It ran off Martin Luther King Parkway and it was near where she used to live. It catered to university students There were several apartment complexes and a grouping of all the fast food places. Parked outside his address was a red Ford fiesta which immediately answered one question. Billy had not driven his car to Sandy Shoals.

The car was locked. She parked beside it and used the keys the mayor had given her to open the driver's side door. The inside of the car was a little messy with books and a jacket thrown carelessly in the back seat and an empty fast food bag on the passenger side. An empty coffee mug, horribly stained, was in a cup holder. The dashboard held the car's manual and Billy's proof of insurance. Nothing else.

There was nothing under the seats. The trunk was empty except for the spare tire.

She shut and locked the door. A slightly plump young woman came out of one of the bottom apartments. She wore tight black leggings that looked as if they were painted on and a top that came to her midriff. She wore platform shoes with thick heels. Not a good look for her body type.

She became aware her ex-husband was standing at her elbow.

"I love the feel of a campus," he said, staring at the young woman.

"You're disgusting," she said. "Even dead, you're disgusting."

The young woman climbed into a car and drove away, without once glancing at Jodi. Late for class, maybe.

She ignored Timothy and walked up the stairs to the apartment building. Called the Bulldog Arms, evidently a tribute to the University of Georgia mascot. Billy's apartment was on the bottom floor near the stairwell that led upstairs. She couldn't shake the feeling she was doing the wrong thing.

She knew there was a risk of contaminating evidence by entering Billy's apartment alone. She knew better. The dull and uninspired monotone of an overweight detective who spread a handling evidence class over three long days was painfully burned into her memory. Proper evidence handling could be the difference between being found guilty or innocent.

Just because she had a hunch Billy was not guilty was not enough to excuse what she was doing.

Despite her misgivings, she opened the door and stepped inside. The apartment was a one-bedroom with a single bath. It had a small living area and kitchen combined. She started in the kitchen first. There were a few cans of Campbell soup in the kitchen pantry and a half-empty jar of peanut butter. The refrigerator was empty except for two bottles of imported ale. The connecting room had a couch, an overstuffed chair, and a flat screen television mounted on the wall. The bathroom closet had a few sets of towels. The small shower had dried soap and a dry washrag hanging on the towel bar. The medicine cabinet was empty. The single bedroom had a queen-sized bed but there was nothing on it but a mattress cover. Sheets and a blanket were folded neatly at the bottom of the bed. The bedroom closet was empty except for a pair of tennis shoes and two pairs of jeans on wire hangars. The dresser had a few sets of underwear and t-shirts, in plastic laundry covers. On top of the dresser was a man's wooden valet. It had space enough for a wallet and watch, but it was empty except for a key fob. The key fob was a specialty item given away to advertise a business called Teal

Automotive, Savannah Georgia.

There was also a photograph. The dead woman and Billy Chutney standing out in front of the Sad Cow Restaurant. For a moment she was tempted to take it. It would be another black mark against Billy, another win in Blankenship's column. But it would truly be tampering with evidence, and she already had a pearl in her pocket that was making her feel guilty enough.

She left the photo where it was.

Timothy had stayed at her elbow the entire time, but he vanished when the front door opened and Harold Blankenship stepped in, accompanied by a uniformed Athens police lieutenant. Blankenship's face was flushed with anger, but the lieutenant looked almost amused. The Athens officer was a slim, nice-looking man named Ed Weller. Jodi had gone through the police academy with him, and it had been Ed that she had sent the photos of the tattoo.

"What are you doing here?" Blankenship demanded.

"I have written permission of the owner to look around," she said. "I suppose you've got a warrant."

"You'd better believe it," he said. "Signed by a judge. You'd better be careful, girlie. Concealing evidence is a crime."

"Girlie?" she questioned.

"I asked you what you were doing here."

Blankenship's voice was getting higher. He was working himself up to a rage. His face was already blood-red.

"Calm yourself, Barney," she said.

Ed Weller laughed and tried to cover it up with a cough.

"You've got no business here," Blankenship said.

"I told you already. I have written permission of the person who pays the rent," she said.

"That doesn't matter. I know why you're here. Concealing

evidence is a crime."

She could have concealed very little in her jeans and pull-over top, but Blankenship was acting as if she had the Mona Lisa in her pocket.

"I can see what you're thinking, and you're not going to search me," she told Blankenship.

"Maybe I could search you," Ed suggested.

"In your dreams," Jodi said.

Blankenship brushed past her, into the single bedroom. She heard him making noises as he started his search. Like an animal rooting.

"You really have written permission, Jodi?" Ed asked.

"Yes."

"Even with written permission, you know better."

She nodded. "Maybe. But Blankenship has the kid convicted and serving time already. Maybe he is guilty, but I'd prefer to have someone investigate who has an open mind."

"And Blankenship doesn't?"

"There's politics involved, Ed," she said.

He nodded in understanding.

They had become friends at the academy. Ed wanted to be closer than friends, but she was still in the process of recovering from her divorce and then her former husband's death, and Ed had accepted her rejection graciously. Now, he wore a brand-new wedding band and a wife at home who was seven months into her pregnancy.

"This is about the dead woman and the photos you sent me?" he asked.

"Yes. But please don't mention to Blankenship about Cat Esterhazy. I'd like a chance to talk to her first."

"I won't unless he asks, and I doubt he'll ask. He hasn't said anything about her tattoos. He seems convinced he's already found her killer. Until you called him Barney, I kept wondering who he reminded me off. And he is the excitable type."

"Billy Chutney might have killed her," Jodi admitted. "I don't have evidence that says he didn't, other than instinct. I just don't think he's the one."

"Sometimes trusting your instinct can be a good idea," Ed said.

A sound came from the bedroom, like a whooping cheer at a football game. It was loud enough to be heard through the closed windows. Jodi sighed. It was too much to hope that even an inept policeman would miss the photograph.

"And things just got worse," Jodi said.

"How?"

"There's proof positive that Billy and the woman were together. There's a picture of them taken in front of the Sad Cow."

"The Sad Cow has something to do with this?" Ed asked, a sudden tension in his voice.

"Possibly," she said.

"That's bad news, Jodi," he said. "The Sad Cow has been associated with illegal gambling, drugs and an escort service."

"The dead woman was older than Billy," Jodi said. "I wonder if she could have been an escort?"

"Odds are good that she was if she knew the Petak brothers," Ed said.

"Brothers? I never knew of one Petak. Boris."

"Bede Petak was the younger brother. He made the mistake a couple of years ago of getting caught with a concealed weapon. He served some time in Reidsville, and then he came back here for a while. But then he disappeared. Rumor is the brothers had a disagreement and Bede moved to someplace on the coast. Seattle, I think."

"The farther away, the better," Jodi said. "Do you think Boris is still running an escort service?"

Ed shrugged. “We haven’t been able to prove it, but the department suspects he is.”

Jodi shrugged. "Billy might have been a client. But it's odd."

"What?"

"I don't think Billy was living here. At least not all the time. There’s not enough of his clothes. The place just doesn't look lived in. Not by a college student."

"So where was he living?"

"With her, maybe?"

"Then that doesn't sound like a business proposition," Ed said. "More like a relationship. You're thinking true love. This is not some kind of silly romantic movie. Love affairs between escorts and clients don't happen."

"She could have been experienced enough to make Billy think it was love," Jodi said.

"And if he found out the hard truth, he might have been upset," Ed suggested.

"Upset enough to kill," Jodi said.

25.

The tattoo parlor was in a small red brick building in a shopping center called Bulldog Square. It was an aging group of buildings that had once held a Walmart but now had several shops in a row. None of them were brand names. A vape shop, the tattoo parlor, a shop advertising exotic herbal remedies, and a Greek restaurant. The Greek restaurant took up most of the space. It looked popular. It was early for lunch, but people were crowded inside. Jodi found herself thinking of a Greek chicken wrap with peppers and cucumbers and garlic.

The garlic in a good wrap lingered for hours, but she wasn't planning on kissing anyone soon.

She had a momentary thought about how Geoff would kiss. She shook her head violently to get it out of her head. Not good thinking such things.

Entering the tattoo parlor, she remembered it but the overweight man sitting in the chair was unfamiliar. He looked up from the magazine he was reading and smiled.

"You are a tall one," he said. "You want a nice butterfly. I could do a nice small one on your cheek."

Even if she had desired a butterfly, she would have never allowed this man to get near her with a needle. He looked grungy. His hair was long and greasy, and he had deep pockmarks on his face. He wore a black t-shirt and his heavy arms were covered with ink.

"I was looking for Cat Esterhazy," she said.

He shook his head in disgust. "The boss only does appointments, and she doesn't do many of those anymore. Besides, she charges a lot. You can get a little butterfly from me at half the price and I can do just as good a job. I'm an artist."

"I'm sure you are," Jodi said, "but I still need to talk to Cat."

"You'll find her next door, at the herbalist place," he said, and went back to his magazine.

The place next door was called Catnip. Fitting. A bell rang as she entered, but there was nobody out front. The shelves were filled with bottles with no labels. It smelled musty. It was no GNC. It reminded her more of the witch's house in a fairy tale.

The woman who stepped through the back room could have been the witch. She was tall and lean. Black hair swept down to her waist. Her eyes were just as black and brooding. She wore no makeup. She wore black jeans and a black t-shirt and knee-high leather boots. The blood red dagger on her arm was frightful looking, and so were the red flames that crept up her neck. She wore three gold studs in her left ear. Nothing in her right.

She did not smile.

"Five-0," she said.

Jodi nodded. "It's been a long time, Cat."

"Not nearly long enough, sweetie," Cat said. Cat leaned against the counter. "I always thought you should have been a dancer. Like that video, you were in. The Dancing Girl. You had some moves, honey. You're wasted as a campus cop."

"I don't work for the university anymore," Jodi said. "I work for another department now. Near the seashore."

"Good for you," Cat said. "What can I do for Five-0? Something to make you less cranky. Perhaps something to revitalize your love-life?"

"I want to ask you about a tattoo," she said.

Cat shrugged. "I don't do the ink anymore. Not much. Unless

somebody really has a lot to offer. You look like you might have a lot to offer."

"I'm just a broke police officer," Jodi said.

"I wasn't talking about money," Cat said.

Jodi cleared her throat, but before she could say anything, Cat turned and went through hanging curtains and disappeared. Jodi followed. A single small room was beyond the curtains. It smelled of burning incense. The walls were an off-white color. There were no windows. A single bare light bulb lit the room, but it left a lot of shadows. It was a little like a jail cell.

The only furniture was a small table and a couple of chairs. A small refrigerator in the corner gave off a steady hum. Cat slumped at the table.

"I don't really want to have a conversation with Five-0," Cat said.

"I found a dead woman on a beach in Sandy Shoals, Georgia," Jodi said.

Cat shrugged.

"She had a tattoo," Jodi said. "A big butterfly across her back with some little butterflies making up some of the wings. It was intricately done. By a real artist."

For the first time Cat looked interested.

"I think you did the tattoo," Jodi said. "Maybe you've got some records, or maybe you could remember who she was if I showed you the tattoo. Maybe you could help us with a name. Her fingerprints don't show up anywhere. Maybe she's got family somewhere. People who would like to know what happened to her."

"I did a lot of tattoos," Cat said.

"I just have the feeling that this one was special," Jodi said.

She scrolled to the photographs on her phone and showed

them to Cat.

Jodi was unprepared for how Cat reacted. Her eyes rolled back in her head and she slumped in her chair. She went to the floor and Jodi was just quick enough to catch her head before it slammed forcefully on the cement. It only lasted for a second and then Cat's color returned, and her eyes opened. It took another for her dark eyes to focus.

"What happened?" she asked

"You fainted," Jodi said.

She shook her head. "I don't faint."

"Nevertheless," Jodi said.

"Water in the fridge," she said. "I'm suddenly dry."

Jodi found bottled water in the small refrigerator, unscrewed the top and put it down in front of her. Cat gulped it noisily and finished the bottle quickly. She hurled the empty plastic bottle into a metal trashcan in the corner.

"Who was she, Cat?" Jodi asked.

"She was my half-sister," Cat said.

Cat put the closed sign on the door, and they went next door to the Greek restaurant. There were people waiting at the door, but Cat ignored them and led Jodi to an empty booth in the back. Cat seemed oblivious to the ugly looks she got, and Jodi tried to ignore them.

A waitress came over immediately.

"You want the special, Ms. Esterhazy?" the waitress asked.

"Yes," Cat said. "And give Five-0 here whatever she wants."

Jodi couldn't resist the savory smells, but she took pity on the people around her and she ordered the chicken wrap but without the garlic or the potatoes. She ordered tea.

"You seem to get special service," Jodi said.

"I own the place," Cat said casually. "I own the block. All the shops."

The food came quickly. Cat had some sort of lamb with the potatoes, but she only picked at it. Jodi took a big bite of her wrap. She didn't think it was as tasty as the one she used to get at the store beside her apartment in Athens, but perhaps it was because she had left the garlic off.

"Tell me about her," Jodi asked.

“Her name is Donna. Same dad. Different momma. My mom died when I was three and Dad married again. I had trouble with my stepmother, especially after Donna was born. I ran away a couple of times. When I was fifteen, I ran away for the last time. Donna was ten.”

“How did you manage?” Jodi asked.

Cat shrugged. “I spent some time on the streets. I survived. I discovered I was a good artist, and I started doing ink. I ended up opening my own shop in Athens. I hadn’t heard from Donna in years until she walked into my shop one day. I didn’t think we’d get along, but we did. She had dreams of being a lawyer. She came to my apartment a dozen times and we talked and drank wine. She met my friends, and she introduced me to my dad again. It was hard but we worked some things out. I even found myself being polite to my stepmother.”

Jodi did some mental calculations. Cat looked in her late thirties, but some of her appearance could have been attributed to a rough life. It would make Donna somewhere in her late twenties or early thirties, maybe only a year or two older than Jodi.

“You said she wanted to be a lawyer?” Jodi asked. “How did she end up...” She left the rest of her question unasked.

Cat nodded in understanding. “Dad dropped dead of a heart attack and everything changed. Donna was crazy about Dad. After the funeral, her grades suffered. She seldom smiled. She drank a little too much wine when she was with me. She told me one night she had met someone."

"Someone on campus?" Jodi asked.

Jodi sensed an odd hesitancy before Cat answered. "I never knew for certain. Then she stopped coming around. I should have checked with her but by then my butterflies were getting popular. I stayed busy. I had a chance to do some others. I got into herbs and natural remedies. I kind of lost track of her."

"When did you see her again?"

"She came walking into the tattoo shop again. She wanted a tattoo. I almost didn't recognize her."

Cat started to take a bite of her lamb and then put her fork down. "Her hair was long and blond. She had on too much makeup. Her skirt was short, and she wasn't wearing a bra. She looked older, harder, and cheap. I told her so. You know what she answered?"

"What?" Jodi asked.

"She said she sure wasn't cheap," Cat answered. "Just ask around and I'd find out. I thought she might have meant it as joke, but I gave her the tattoo she wanted."

"The butterfly on her back," Jodi asked.

"Yes," Cat answered. "And then I asked around. She had dropped out of school. And she was working for an escort service."

"The Petak brothers?" Jodi asked.

Cat nodded. "Yes. But you didn't hear that from me. Nobody around here messes with Boris Petak. He's bad news."

"Couldn't you convince Donna to go back to school, or go back home? Anything?"

"I tried, but it wasn't the same Donna. It was like a black hole where her heart used to be. I think it had a lot to do with who she met after Dad died. He influenced her, and I think he eventually pimped her to the Petak brothers."

"Are you sure you don't know who it was?"

"No," Cat said, shaking her head vehemently but again Jodi sensed a hesitancy, something left unsaid. "But I suspect it was an older guy, someone who was steady and dependable on the outside. A father figure."

"Like a professor?" Jodi asked.

"Possibly," Cat said.

Her answer still seemed evasive, and her eyes flickered away almost immediately. Jodi was sure Cat knew more than what she was saying, perhaps the identity of Donna's professor, but she decided not to push. She had already found out more than she expected.

"When was the last time you saw your sister," Jodi said.

"She came in a few months ago to tell me she was moving. She would let me know her address. I tried to convince her to stay, to come to work for me. She said she couldn't stay in Athens. She was making a lifestyle change."

"And she never contacted you after that?" Jodi asked.

"No. Maybe she did contact her mom. I don't know."

"You think it's all right if I go and talk with her mother," Jodi said.

"Fine with me. I'll give you her address in Conyers. To tell you the truth, I don't want to call her. I called her soon after Donna left to see if Donna had told her where she was living. She hadn't. And I was practically cussed out for Donna going astray. I guess it's always that way."

"What do you mean?"

"You have to blame someone."

26.

Her cell phone rang as she turned onto US-78 in Monroe, Georgia.

"How are things going?" Dr. Theo asked.

"I'm finding things out," Jodi replied. "I don't know if what I'm finding out will help Billy or not."

"Hopefully, it will. The lynch mob is gathering."

"Things are that bad?"

"The sheriff plans on holding a press conference tomorrow. Not at the county, but on the courthouse steps in Sandy Shoals. Adding insult to injury."

"Barney's probably already called the Sheriff about finding a picture of Billy and the dead girl," Jodi said.

"That's not good," Dr. Theo said.

"No." Jodi sighed. "Is Billy still in a coma?"

"Yes, but he's showing signs of waking up. Once he's awake, I can't protect him long. Especially if It's been proven he actually knew the dead woman."

Jodi let out her breath. "I think it was a financial arrangement."

Dr. Theo gasped. "That's not going to help Sunni's state of mind. I've put her on medication. She's a wreck."

"I haven't taken any medication, and I feel like a wreck," Jodi said.

"That's because you haven't stopped since you got back to

Sandy Shoals," Dr. Theo said. "Are you planning on being back this evening?"

Jodi sensed something more than curiosity in Dr. Theo's question.

"It's my plan," she said. "It'll probably be late. Why?"

"I'll see you then," Dr. Theo said, and rang off.

Jodi was certain something else was going on, but Dr. Theo wasn't going to talk about it over the phone. She hoped it was not another attempt to get her to mend bridges with Kate and her dad.

Jodi tried to shake off her growing irritation with Dr. Theo's meddling, and tried to concentrate on the traffic. There was plenty of it. When she was a girl, her father had brought her and Kate to Stone Mountain for the day. Even then, there was a lot less traffic and few buildings. There had even been a few fields covered in scrub pine and with a few broken chimneys sticking up out of the weeks from abandoned farmhouses. Her dad told them that even when he was a boy, there had still been a few working farms and fields thick with cotton. All that had been replaced by strip malls, restaurants, gas stations and convenience stores. Progress.

It was late afternoon when she reached Conyers.

Restaurants, banks and grocery stores cluttered up the drive and traffic bad. She turned off Highway 138 at the Walgreen's drug store and followed it to the turn on Ebenezer Road. The house she was looking for was on the left side of Ebenezer, a dark brick with green shutters across the street from a church.

The woman who opened the door was not quite as tall as Jodi, and rail thin. Her brown hair was stringy and hung to her shoulders and her dark eyes were as hard as flint and full of suspicion at the stranger at the door. Jodi was hoping Cat might have called, but evidently, she hadn't.

"What is it?" the woman said.

"I'm Jodi Weathers," she said. "I'm police chief of Sandy Shoals, Georgia. I need to talk to Joan Esterhazy."

"You're a police chief?" the woman said, disbelief in her voice. She looked over Jodi's clothes, and then disbelievingly at the patrol car in the driveway. "You have some kind of identification?"

"Actually, I don't," Jodi said. "I haven't been police chief long."

Technically, she still wasn't sure if she was officially police chief, but it didn't seem the moment to go into a lot of detail.

"I have my business cards from my job with the campus police in Athens," Jodi said. "And my driver's license. Are you Joan?"

The woman shook her head. "I'm Ruth Collins. I'm Joan's sister. Can I see one of those cards?"

Ruth was just as suspicious as she looked. Jodi showed her the card.

"It's about Donna," Jodi said.

"You know Donna?" Ruth asked. "We've been kind of worried. She doesn't visit often but she phones regular. She hasn't phoned in a while. What kind of bad news?

Jodi would have preferred to give her information to the mother, but there was no way to avoid answering.

“I’m afraid we found a body on the beach at Sandy Shoals,” Jodi said. “We believe it’s Donna. I talked to her sister Cat already. She gave me this address. Unfortunately, Donna’s fingerprints aren’t in the system. We had no way of identifying her except some tattoos.”

Ruth nodded. “She had those, all right. Cat did them Cat’s an artist with the needle I guess you’d better come in.”

Ruth led her through the house into a back room. It was a pleasant, airy room with lots of windows, but there wasn't much outside to see. Only other houses. A small, frail woman sat in a wheelchair watching a flat-screen television with the sound off. She looked up at Jodi, her eyes bright and curious.

"She's come with news about Donna," Ruth said.

"You know my Donna?" Joan said.

Jodi didn't answer right away. Her mouth felt dry. Her eyes were drawn to a nearby table with many framed photographs. Several were the image of the dead woman. Donna Esterhazy standing next to a middle-aged man by a semi-truck. Probably her father. Donna in cheerleader costume. Donna in hat and gown. Donna in her Easter outfit standing outside the house. Donna and a nervous looking young man.

Not one picture of Cat.

"I knew it would be bad news," Joan said. "Is she dead?"

Ruth nodded without speaking.

"Someone killed her," Joan said.

"Why would you say that?" Jodi asked.

"I'm old, but I'm not stupid," Joan said. "I know my daughter changed. I knew what she was doing to get all those flashy clothes and that fancy car she drove."

"If anyone killed her, it was that professor," Ruth said.

"What professor?" Jodi asked.

"She was involved with a professor, and he was a sorry individual. He took our sweet Donna and turned her into someone we didn't even recognize. He took advantage. She was all messed up when her daddy died, and he gave her a shoulder to cry on. And Donna was way out of her league. An older man. Like a father figure. He took her dad's place and then dumped her. Like so much garbage."

"You know the name of the professor?" Jodi asked.

"No," Ruth answered. "But you ask Cat. Cat knew his name."

Which was odd because Cat had claimed not to know.

"She left school after the professor dumped her. She told us she transferred to an art school in Savannah, but I always knew better. I wasn't sure until now that her mother knew what was going on."

The frail woman was listening to them both intently, but Jodi wasn't sure how much she could understand.

"You think she got back with this professor and he killed her," Jodi said. "Why?"

"She came around last, about six months ago. And she was as happy as I'd seen her. She was doing her hair different again. Back the color it was. An she was softer somehow. She acted like she was in love, and I just figured she was back with that no-account professor. Maybe he dumped her again, and this time he resisted. Maybe she threatened to tell his wife."

"If you don't know his name or anything else about him, how do you know he was married?" Jodi asked.

"That type is always married," Ruth said harshly.

It was a possibility. Even if it were far-fetched, a good defense attorney could shed some doubt by introducing the professor into the trial. If she could find him? But there was also a possibility that her new happiness was because of her relationship with Billy Chutney.

"Are you sure you never heard his name?"

"No but I told you. Cat knows."

It looked like she was going to have to make yet another trip to Athens and confront Cat about the name Cat supposedly didn't know.

"You said Donna had a fancy car? What kind?"

"A Lexus," Ruth said. "A blue convertible. It looked really expensive."

"Was she still living in Athens?"

"No," Ruth said. "She moved. She never told us where."

Another dead end.

Jodi took out another of her business cards from the campus police. Her cell number was still correct, but she marked through the address. On the back of the card she wrote down the number for the office of the Sandy Shoals Coroner.

"This is where you can contact the county about arrangements," she told Ruth. "And this is my cell. I mentioned I'm no longer with the campus police. Please contact me if you can of think of anything else."

Jodi prepared to leave, and the frail woman put her hand on Jodi's arm. "The photo album," she said.

Ruth looked confused for a moment and then gave Jodi an embarrassed shrug. "I guess she saw you looking at the pictures, and she wants you to look at the ones in the photo album. Family stuff."

It was late and Jodi wanted to get on the road, but she didn't know how to politely refuse, and Ruth pulled a large, heavy book down from a nearby shelf. Ruth placed it in her sister's lap, and Jodi got ready to look at a lot of pictures from the past. Instead Eula opened the album up in the middle and tapped a picture in the center. It was Donna Esterhazy.

With a man.

"Him?" Joan said.

"Is that him?" Ruth asked. "I didn't know there was a picture."

"I doubted he knew it was taken," Jodi said.

"I'm still betting he was the one who killed her," Ruth said. "Find him. The pig. He's the one."

"No," Joan said softly. "He certainly was a pig, but he didn't kill her."

"How can you be sure?" Ruth asked.

"Because he died a few years ago," Jodi said.

Jodi didn't mention she was once married to him.

"It's not fair," Timothy said. "I get blamed for everything."

He was sulking. He sat slouched in the far corner of the pick-up; his arms folded across his desk. He had appeared almost as soon as she had climbed tiredly into the truck.

"Are you trying to tell me you're innocent?" Jodi asked.

"I was a good man," he insisted. "Okay, I might have liked the ladies, but that doesn't make me some kind of pervert."

"I think the word was pig," Jodi said. "It seems to fit."

"You're being harsh," Timothy said.

He kept protesting for most of the ride back to Shoals. It was blessed relief when he vanished.

27.

It was nearly ten in the evening before she got back to the house on Baker Street. The rain had stopped on her trip to Athens but as soon as she turned on 17, it came back again. The same slow drizzle Jodi had been living with for days.

A car was parked in her driveway, and a shadowy figure sat in the porch swing. Jodi didn't recognize Dr. Theo until she drew close.

"Another long night," Dr. Theo said.

"Seems to be the norm," Jodi said.

"Blankenship is acting like a jackass," Dr Theo said. "The Chutneys are past hysteria. There's now a uniformed officer at Billy's door. The sheriff keeps making veiled threats that he's going to charge Billy in the press conference tomorrow."

"It just gets better and better," Jodi said.

"Do you think Billy did it?"

"I'm not sure what I think," Jodi said. "Nobody's been able to talk to Billy. We don't know his version of what happened. All we know for certain was that Billy and the woman were at the Tavern. Maybe not at the same time."

"But you think they were?" Dr. Theo said.

"I'm afraid they were. I also found out who the woman was and I'm going to have to inform the sheriff. When he discovers who she was, there may be a paper trail or even witnesses who can put them together. Either in Athens or Savannah."

"Your homecoming hasn't been all that pleasant," Dr. Theo

commented.

Jodi shrugged.

"Have you any idea what you will do next?"

Jodi shook her head. For a time, the two women sat quietly. She figured Dr. Theo hadn't shown up on her porch after midnight to talk about politics. Sooner or later Dr. Theo would get around to what she wanted. In the meantime, Jodi thought about a nice long, hot shower and her soft bed waiting.

"It's politics," Dr. Theo said finally. "It's all politics. Arresting Billy would put a feather in the sheriff's cap, and maybe he could shut down the city police department. He'd like that."

"It's possible Billy is guilty," Jodi said.

"I know," Dr. Theo admitted. "And if he is, we'll all have to accept it. But if he isn't, I'd hate to see him convicted because of politics."

"I never had to deal with politics much with the campus police," Jodi said. "I don't care for it much. The real question should only be guilt or innocence."

"True," Dr. Theo said. "But I learned long ago that real life isn't that black and white. Too many variables. Sort of like the relationship you have with your dad and Kate."

Here it comes, Jodi thought.

"I'm really tired, and I've told you already that is not a conversation I want to have."

"I understand your anger," Dr. Theo said. "Believe me. But you've been angry for a long time. It's time for a little forgiveness to seep in."

Jodi shook her head in disgust. "I'm going inside. I need a shower."

She stood up.

"Sit down," Dr. Theo said sharply.

Jodi sat.

“You remember the day you brought Billy into the hospital and your father and Geoff were outside?”

“I remember.”

“Your father said Kate was there to see me. For a check-up.”

“I had a feeling he wasn’t telling the complete truth,” Jodi said.

“He wasn’t.”

“There’s something wrong with Kate?” Jodi asked.

She was surprised at her own sudden intensity of emotion.

"Kate had a miscarriage during the storm," Dr. Theo said softly. "She was five months pregnant."

28.

The damage to the marina was worse than her father had let on.

The gate to the marina was gone. The storm had evidently blown it into the Atlantic. An overturned Chris-Craft was just beyond the entrance. A portion of the dock lights were out, and all the boats were in deep shadow. There was only a concrete slab where the bait shop had been.

She parked outside the building and she could hear the hum of the main generator. There were a few lights burning in the office.

She sat for a moment, gathering her strength.

She had left Dr. Theo and got back in her car and came immediately to the marina. Now she wasn't sure what she would do or say. She still felt angry. She also felt guilty, as if somehow Kate losing the baby was her fault. Dr. Theo had tried to assure her that it was not, but the assurances didn't help.

The light above the office door came on immediately as she got out of her car, and her dad opened the front door before she reached it. He didn't say anything. She thought he looked older than his years. He stepped aside and let her enter the spacious front room. How many years had she spent her afternoons standing behind the desk, greeting the boaters, signing in their forms? Everything was painfully familiar except the new flat screen television mounted on a wall.

He looked at her with a mixture of curiosity and apprehension.

"It's okay, Dad. I've come to see Kate. I'm not going to get hysterical. Dr. Theo told me about the baby."

"Then you know she doesn't need any more stress right now," he said.

"Dr. Theo said my seeing her might help," Jodi said. "I promise not to yell at her, Dad. I won't lie and say I'm suddenly okay with everything, but Kate and I can at least be civilized. And I'm terribly sorry about the baby."

"It was a boy," her dad said.

His misery was evident. There was nothing she could say.

"I'll make coffee," he said.

She went past him and down the hallway, past the showers and changing rooms and through the swinging doors marked private. Her room had been the first one on the right. The door was shut. She opened it and flipped on the light.

It was being changed into a nursery. There was already a crib and new wallpaper with bunny rabbits covered one half a section of wall. The rest of the wallpaper was in a roll leaning against the corner. Work interrupted. For the worst reason of all.

She felt a surge of anger. Her father and Kate moving her out of their lives as quickly as possible. Even as she felt the heat, she knew she was being irrational. Common sense took over. Of course, they were changing her old room to nursery. There was limited space. It had nothing to do with her.

She turned the lights back off and closed the door. She leaned against it for a moment. She was tempted to turn around. She wasn't ready for this. She had held onto her anger and hurt for too long. Every step down the rest of the hallway seemed begrudging.

She knocked on the doorway at the end of the hall. There was no answer. She waited a moment and then she opened it and stepped in. This room had also changed. There was no longer a masculine flavor to it. The walls had been repainted a light blue. The single bed her father had slept in had been changed to a queen-sized.

Kate sat propped up on pillows in the middle of the bed. She wore a dark blue nightgown. Her eyes were open, but she didn't see Jodi. It was as if she was looking at something far away, something nobody else could see.

"Kate," Jodi said.

It all came back to her then, a painful rush of memories. The first day they met. In elementary school. Kate Morelli was five years older than Jodi and wrongly diagnosed with learning difficulties. She had been held back four grades and ended up in Jodi's class. If there had been some sort of special needs class at Sandy Shoals, Kate would have been part of it. She was reading on a second-grade level, and had trouble forming words.

She was small, dark, painfully shy. When Jodi found a couple of girls bullying her one afternoon after school, reducing her to tears, Jodi rushed in, both fists swinging. She got detention, a note to her dad, and a new best friend.

They were an odd couple. Jodi, taller than any kid in her school, a rawboned, skinny, redheaded tomboy, and the short, shy, sweet and socially inept daughter of alcoholic parents.

Around town people believed it was something of a miracle because seemingly overnight Kate's skills improved, she became more outgoing. She started testing higher and educators realized it was a more of an emotional problem than an educational one.

Despite the difference in their ages, they became like sisters.

Looking at her, Jodi got the same feeling she got when the older girls were picking on her. Kate looked fragile, defenseless. Some wounds didn't show as much on the outside, but they went terribly deep.

"Kate," Jodi said again.

Kate turned her head and saw her. Her eyes focused.

"Hello, Jodi," Kate said.

Jodi felt the need to take her friend into her arms and hug her tightly, but she had been angry for too long. It was hard to let it all go. She took a step and hesitated. How many times had they sat together on a bed and talked about their two favorite subjects, boys and boats? How many dreams had they shared? They had talked of careers and fashions and their favorite movie stars, and now and then they had talked of finding husbands.

Jodi had never expected the one Kate found to be her dad.

29.

Jodi woke to a text on her phone from Frances.

"Meeting with the sheriff and Geoff at courthouse. 9ish."

She rolled over. She had fallen asleep on the bed. Kate was curled up, hugging a pillow, in deep sleep. Careful not to disturb her, Jodi slipped out of the room. She showered in the customer bath and reluctantly put her same clothes back on. She still felt a little grimy, and deep-bone tired. She had slept for only a few hours, after spending a long time with Kate. They didn't talk. A few whispered words and then long periods of silence.

She found her dad asleep on the couch in the reception area. She wrote him a note.

"Have a meeting. Be back for lunch. I'll buy."

It was a little after eight when she drove past the broken marina gate. She had wanted to spend the morning with her dad and Kate. There was still a of things that needed to be said. The night before, she had promised Kate they would take the Gypsy out again. If one thing could heal, it would be the Gypsy.

Twenty minutes later, she parked in the county courthouse parking area, and found Frances pacing back and forth in front of the courthouse steps.

"What's going on?" Jodi said.

"Theo told Geoff that you knew who the dead woman is."

"I was going to give that information to Blankenship today," Jodi protested.

"I think Geoff has something else in mind," Frances said.

The county Sheriff was slender and nice-looking dressed in an expensive looking gray suit, dark blue shirt and tie. He was in his sixties with a thick head of dark hair going gray at the temples. Jodi wondered if he used hair color for the gray. It was just a little too perfect.

Harold Blankenship looked rumpled next to him. She felt as tired as Harold looked. Was she ever going to sleep the entire night again?

Geoffrey wore jeans and a black t-shirt with a picture of the characters from Doctor Who on the front. The Sheriff had brought his own secretary to the meeting, a very attractive brunette.

"No need for two people to take notes," the Sheriff announced. "Frances can go back to whatever you have her doing."

"I'd prefer Ms. San to stay," Geoff Hamilton said. “I asked her to take notes. I want to make sure we all agree on what’s said.”

Frances grinned.

The sheriff made a face but then shrugged. Jodi already knew their conversation was also being recorded and probably filmed. She was sure the county had people who could make their technical stuff work properly.

"You asked for this meeting," the sheriff said.

"Jodi has information that she wants to share with you,” Geoff said.

"What kind of information?" Blankenship asked.

"For one thing, I know who our victim was," Jodi said.

The sheriff’s face grew dark and threatening. "You know, and you didn't share it with us?"

"I'm sharing it now," Jodi said. "I didn't know for sure until yesterday evening. Her mother might have contacted the county coroner by now."

"And how did you find this information out?" the sheriff asked.

"Through good investigative work," Geoff interrupted. "She noticed a tattoo on the woman's back, which your Detective didn't think was important. First, because he thought it was suicide and then he ignored it because he was sure Billy Chutney was guilty. She did what your Detective should have done. She found the person that did the tattoo and then she found out our victim's name and then found the mom and an aunt. Her name was in the data base. We now have an address, in Savannah, and we know the kind of car she drove. We'd like an alert sent out on the car."

"All right," the sheriff said, glancing at Blankenship with sour expression. Blankenship stared at Jodi like a deer caught in the headlights. If there had ever been a possibility of Jodi and Blankenship being friends, it was gone forever.

"These are things you could have found out for yourself if Blankenship wasn't so convinced Billy Chutney killed that woman," Geoff pointed out.

"Okay, you found the address and I admit that's good police work," the sheriff said begrudgingly. "But none of this means Billy Chutney isn't guilty."

"Maybe not," Geoff said. But I'd advise waiting until you search before you make the grandstand play and charge Billy in this afternoon's press conference."

Jodi gave Geoff a look of surprise. There was a sound in his voice she hadn't heard before. She kept thinking of him as a big sleepy bear, but now a tough side was showing through. No wonder Frances thought he was good lawyer.

"I never said I was going to charge him," the sheriff said evasively.

"I'd also like to be assured Chief Weathers is included in the search, and all information is shared with her," Geoff said.

"Or what?" Blankenship interrupted.

"Or the entire county will know that you're an incompetent buffoon," Geoff said.

“Chief Weathers will be included in everything,” the sheriff said quickly, again with a sour look toward Blankenship.

Blankenship started to say something else, but the sheriff cut him off by abruptly standing. "Okay. Blankenship will get the warrants in order. He'll call you when he's set to go. I'll need to see you in my office, Harold, before you leave."

The sheriff left, followed hurriedly by his attractive secretary. Blankenship followed a little slower.

"How do you spell buffoon?" Frances San asked.

Jodi dissolved into laughter.

30.

The sheriff didn't even turn up for the press conference.

Instead, Howard Blankenship met with reporters on the Sandy Shoals courthouse steps, and he never even mentioned Billy Chutney. He talked about how the investigation was progressing, and he shocked Jodi by giving her credit for finding the name of the victim. He gave a description of the car the victim drove and said warrants were in process to search the victim's Savannah apartment.

Jodi had mixed feelings about the press conference. She was glad the sheriff and the district attorney still felt there wasn't enough evidence to charge Billy, but she didn't like everyone knowing the woman's name. If Billy was not guilty, if there was another killer out there, he or she might be hiding their tracks.

After leaving the station, she had told Frances she was going home to change clothes, and then pick up lunch and return to the marina.

Her phone rang as soon as she got into her car.

"He's awake," Dr. Theo said.

She didn't need to ask who.

"Who else knows?" Jodi asked.

"Just you and Geoff," Dr. Theo said. "But I'm about to call his parents."

"I need to talk to him first," Jodi said. "Without his parents. He'll never answer a single question in front of his mother."

"I don't know how that would be possible," Dr. Theo said

reluctantly. Then. "I'm going to have another MRI run. There's a waiting room just outside the room where the machine is. It's room 12 on the third floor. One of the nurses will leave him there while the technicians get ready. You won't have long."

“Give me fifteen minutes,” Jodi said.

She parked her car on a side road two blocks from the hospital. She figured there would be reporters around, and they would flock to a police car. She was right. Two news vans were in front of the hospital and a reporter was giving an interview on the front steps. Jodi slipped through a side door.

Inside, the news was being broadcast from a television mounted on the wall in the reception area. A serious looking anchorman from a Savannah station was having a conversation with his newscast partner, a cute blond with dimples and a practiced smile. Billy Chutney’s name was mentioned several times. The television flashed to pictures of Billy, of the Mayor and Sunni, and Geoff Hamilton.

Evidently the Sheriff avoiding the press conference had not stopped the gossip.

Jodi groaned as a familiar video started playing. The newscaster's voice droned behind it.

"The victim was identified earlier today by the new police chief of Sandy Shoals," the announcer spoke. "Those of us who lived in the area will always remember chief Jodi Weathers as The Dancing Girl."

Jodi walked faster, catching only bits and pieces of the rest of the story. A small boy in a chair near the television seemed transfixed by the video, and then his eyes widened as he noticed Jodi. His mother sat beside him reading a magazine and he started tugging at her arm. Jodi hoped she was out of sight before the mother looked up.

A Sheriff's deputy was still stationed in front of Billy's door.

Well, what did she think, that she was just going to be allowed to walk in?

Her phone rang again. "It's set up. Third floor. You won't have long."

"I knew you could do it," Jodi said.

"How did things go with Kate?" Dr. Theo said.

"We're trying to work things out," Jodi said. "I'm going by again for lunch."

Silence on the phone Dr. Theo never said goodbye.

Jodi took the stairs. She didn't want to run into anybody she knew or reporters who might recognize her. The third floor was practically deserted, and she found the room with no problem. Through the windows of the swinging doors she could see the MRI machine and a woman behind a glass-in enclosure.

Exactly five minutes later a male nurse rolled Billy into the room. Billy was awake, but he didn't look healthy. A huge bandage nearly covered the side of his head.

"Who are you?" he asked Jodi suspiciously.

"I'm Chief Weathers," she said.

"You're the girl," he said. "The Dancing Girl. The one in the green bathing suit. It's been all over the television since I woke up."

She shook her head in exasperation. "We don't have a lot of time, Billy. You need to tell me about Donna."

"About who?"

Jodi rolled her eyes. "Donna Esterhazy. You met her at the Sad Cow. I think you might have been in love with her. I don't think you killed her."

Billy started to speak, but then stopped. His eyes were defiant.

"Please, Billy," Jodi said. "You're in a lot of trouble. Your parents are sick with worry about you."

"My mother only thinks I'm going to embarrass her," Billy said.

"I'm sorry Donna is dead, Billy," Jodi said. "But you're going to have to tell me what happened."

Billy looked away.

"I met her mother and her aunt," Jodi said. "Her aunt mentioned that Donna had been different lately. Happier. Like a burden had been lifted from her shoulders. Her aunt Helen thought she might have met somebody special. I think it was you."

Tears glistened in Billy's eyes.

"Please, Billy," she said. "Tell me everything you remember."

"I loved her," Billy said. "I wouldn't have hurt her."

"I believe you, Billy. What happened that night?"

Billy looked defiant again. "We were going to get married."

Jodi tried to keep her expression blank. The idea of Billy going against his mother's wishes for long and marrying an older woman, and a former escort, was ludicrous. Sunni was the stronger personality. She would have eventually worn him down.

But Jodi had him talking and she didn't want to shatter his romantic illusions.

"Tell me how you met her," Jodi said. "Was it at the Sad Cow?"

"They used to give parties after hours at the Sad Cow. There were always girls there. The first time I went, I didn't know what to expect. I was introduced. She called herself Monique. I never met anybody so beautiful, so alive."

"Without having to hear a lot of intimate details," Jodi said. "Was money exchanged?"

He flushed with sudden embarrassment. "I knew before I went that I was expected to pay a fee. It was all handled tastefully."

"How?" Jodi asked.

"It was called club fees," Jodi said. "It was collected each time you visited. Ahead of time. After you had visited the first time, you could request the company of a particular girl."

"And you always requested Donna."

He nodded. "There were rules. I wasn't supposed to ever see her except on the night of the parties. But we started seeing each other every chance we got. It wasn't about money anymore. We fell in love. I found out she was an art student. What she really wanted to do was paint. She wanted to go to Paris and study."

"And you said you would take her after you two were married?"

He nodded.

"Were you living with her?" Jodi asked.

"Yes. I had to keep the apartment in Athens for a while. I still went to my classes. Donna insisted. She didn't want me to drop out of school because of her."

"You stayed in Savannah with her?" Jodi asked.

"Mostly," Billy said.

She didn't want to ask the next question because she was afraid Billy would get offended and stop talking, but the question had to be asked. "How was she earning a living in Savannah?"

Billy lifted his head off the pillow again. "I know what you're thinking, but it wasn't like that. She wasn't doing that anymore. She said she sold her jewelry and she was getting some help from her family."

"And you gave her money," Jodi said.

"All that I could," he admitted.

Billy was fooling himself. Jodi suspected Donna was still involved in being an escort, and just stringing Billy along. For what? Did she really expect Billy would marry her and take her to Paris? Did she have any kind of feelings for Billy at all?

Or was she happy not because she had met someone to love, but because Billy was promising to make her dreams come true?

"What happened the night of the storm?" Jodi asked.

He shook his head. "I really don't remember. It's the truth. Donna wanted to visit the town where I was born. I remember being on the beach with her. I remember how dark it got. I got scared. But then everything went blank. I think I was hit on the head by a sign. I don't remember it clearly. I was in the Tavern when I woke up."

"And Donna was there?" Jodi asked. "Just the two of you?"

"No," he said. "There was someone else. Donna was arguing with him."

"Do you remember who it was?"

"His voice was familiar, but my head hurt bad. I remember that he hit Donna and I got up and tried to help. Whoever it was had a bottle in their hand, and they hit me with it. I heard Donna scream, and then all went black again."

"You don't remember how you ended up in Blackbeard's Tavern?"

"No," he said. "Donna must have gotten me in there somehow."

"Were you drinking?" Jodi asked.

"I had some wine," he said. "Earlier. We had a few beers in the car."

The male nurse returned and there was no time for any more questions, but Billy had given her a lot of things to think about. Nothing proved his innocence or guilt, and there was still the missing gap in his memory.

But at least she knew more than she did.

Which still wasn't much.

The news people caught up to her just outside the hospital, and it was chaos for a while. Rapid-fire questions that she couldn't or wouldn't answer. That frustrated the news people even more. It also irritated her that the news people kept referring to her as The Dancing Girl. High school felt like a long time in the past, and yet she couldn't escape the infamous video.

Andy Warhol was wrong, at least in her case. Her fifteen minutes of fame was going to haunt her forever.

31.

She made it back to her car without stumbling over any more reporters, but she had a phone call as soon as she got inside.

It was Harold 'Barney' Blankenship, and he sounded even more unpleasant than usual. "I'm calling you to let you know we are getting the warrants together to search the woman's apartment. We're meeting with Savannah police there in the morning. Early."

He hung up without telling her how early.

She was hungry and called her dad to tell him she was bringing lunch and would be there in less than thirty minutes. He grunted. She stopped at Scofield's Sandwich and ordered the roast beef, tomato and lettuce with the tiny peppers, on a hunk of sourdough bread. Potato chips to go along, and their special sweet tea.

Her dad was waiting to greet her when she drove into the marina. He took one of her sandwich bags

"Kate's down at the Gypsy," he said. "She said something about you two taking her out again. She looked sort of animated. I haven't seen her that way for a while."

"Things are going to get better, Dad," Jodi promised.

She wasn't sure about her promise. It seemed like every time she thought she was over the hurt; bitter emotions would come crashing back.

Jodi found Kate sitting on the deck near where the Gypsy was docked. The Gypsy looked even older, but well-maintained, a dignified elder. Jodi longed to step on her deck. It would be like hugging an old friend.

Kate's body looked hunched and her pale bare legs hung down. She wore shorts and a shirt that had once had a picture of a bright colored sailing ship. The shirt had faded with time.

"I brought you lunch," Jodi said.

"Scofield's," Kate said. "I haven't had one of their sandwiches in a while."

"And the sweet iced tea," Jodi said.

"Sugar with a little tea in it," Kate said.

Jodi settled beside her.

"You think we can get her ready soon?" Kate asked.

"It'll take some work, but she's a grand old boat. She's never let us down."

Jodi handed over Kate's sandwich. Kate took a bite, but her mind seemed to be on something else other than lunch. They had talked for a long time the evening before, but they had stayed away from sensitive subjects. Like marriage.

"You remember the first time you talked me into going out by ourselves in the Gypsy?" Kate asked.

"I do," Jodi said. "You fell into the water."

"I did not fall," Kate said. " You knew I didn't know all those nautical terms. You could have said push it backwards or forwards, or something in English. I still don't know why you don't call the bow the pointy end. That would make sense."

Jodi laughed. It had been a long time since she had laughed with Kate. It was another thing she missed, and she knew that missing it was mostly her own stubborn fault.

"You think the weather will be okay?" Kate asked.

"We never let weather stop us," Jodi said.

Which wasn't true. They had both been taught to be respectful of the wind and weather, and especially the sea. If Jodi thought it dangerous, she would not have suggested it. But the wind was not bad, and the rain was mostly just irritating. By the time they got the Gypsy ready, it should feel even better.

Kate said something very softly, but her words were caught in the wind.

"What?" Jodi said.

"I'm glad you're here," Kate said. "I'm sorry about everything. I never had a friend like you."

"You going to blubber?" Jodi asked.

"Maybe," Kate answered.

Jodi still wanted to avoid the unpleasant subjects with Kate upset about the baby, but the anger and hurt came bubbling up unexpectedly. Once started, it was like a stone rolling downhill and it couldn't be stopped.

"You were like another daughter," Jodi said harshly. "You were my sister."

"When we were young, that was how it was," Kate agreed. "But then we grew up. You left for college. I was never a college person. I was happier with grease on my hands. I was happier with a paint gun."

"You were happier seducing my father," Jodi said.

Jodi immediately regretted saying it, but it didn't get the response she expected.

Instead of an angry retort, Kate giggled.

"What?"

"Even you can't imagine me seducing your father. Did you picture me in a black nightie dancing like Salome to some sexy music? Me?"

The thought did seem a little crazy, and it almost made her

smile.

“We didn’t mean to fall in love, Jodie. It just happened.”

"And all the time you were coming here, spending the night with me. That trip on the boat to the Bahamas. All that time you were..."

Kate stood and nearly knocked Jodi off the dock into the water. Her face was dark with fury. Jodi went into a defensive stance, but Kate did not swing her arms but came closer and there were tears shimmering in her eyes.

"Other people said nasty things like that, but how could you say it? That article in the Sandy Shoals Tribune with the headline. Robbing the cradle. How did it go? Oh, yeah. Bud practically raised me, along with you. It’s okay for those Hollywood types, but not in Sandy Shoals. People with tiny minds, but how could you even think it? It's disgusting. And even if you could believe it of me, how could you think it of your father?"

"Some men are just susceptible,” Jodi said.

"Susceptible?" Kate said. "Big college word. Is that how you think of your father? As susceptible?"

"Some men are,” Jodi said.

"Maybe that idiot you married was that kind of person, but your father is the smartest, gentlest, hardest-working man I've ever known. And when he proposed, I was in jeans and a sweater and covered in grease from a boat engine. Hollywood romance, right?”

“Okay,” Jodi said. “Maybe susceptible was a bad choice of words.”

Jodi knew what she was hearing was the truth, but perhaps she had always known the truth and was just being hardheaded.

Jodi finished off the last few bites of her sandwich. Kate hadn't taken more than few bites. Jodi gathered up the trash and took it to the nearby trashcan. She noticed Kate's shoulders were shaking. She drew close and saw large tears staining her friend's cheek. Jodi felt a tug of shame. This was her friend and she was hurting.

Jodi sat down and took her into her arms and hugged her tight, rocking her gently.

"I missed you so terribly," Kate said. "I hurt every day you weren't talking to me."

"I'm a stupid, stupid person," Jodi said.

"Yes, you are," Kate agreed.

32.

Donna's address was on a shaded street across from a historic old cemetery. The apartment complex was only one story, and it looked old, but it was well-tended. The only other building on the street was Teal's Garage. It was a big, sprawling complex with a fenced-off area with dozens of automobiles, and more cars out front. It had several bay areas and even so early, half the bays were open. A few men could be seen working inside.

Jodi was the first to arrive. A few moments later a battered green 4x4 pickup pulled up behind her and a uniformed Savannah police sergeant got out. Jodi got out to greet her. The woman was a few years older than Jodi, petite and attractive, with blond hair and wide, expressive green eyes. Despite her being tiny, there was a competent aura about her, a self-assurance that Jodi found herself envying.

"Chief Weathers," she said. "I'm Carol Grady. I understand we're supposed to do a search of a murdered woman's apartment. Do you have the warrants?"

Jodi was surprised because instead of the slow Southern accent she half-expected, Carol sounded English. It was a little incongruous for someone in a Savannah police uniform.

Jodi shook her head. "I'm waiting for someone. A sheriff's detective. He's supposed to have them. I believe that's him now."

Carol heard the tension in Jodi's voice, and she turned to see Harold Blankenship pulling in behind her Volkswagen. Harold slowly climbed out of his car. He had on another of his expensive suits. No hat. Brightly shined shoes. Very spiffy.

He gave Carol the once-over and evidently liked what he saw. He smiled at her. Blankenship smiling was even worse than Blankenship frowning. Introductions were quickly made.

Carol asked for the search warrant and studied it for a moment.

"It says the landlord is Art Teal. I know him. He lives in the last apartment on the end. He's probably not at work yet. We'll go by there and get the key."

The last apartment on the end was opened by a middle-aged man barefoot and in pajama bottoms. His bare chest was covered in thick black hair and he was idly scratching as he opened. Jodi had an immediate sense of familiarity with him, but she was sure she had never met him before.

He looked at Carol in mock alarm. "Is this a raid, Sarge?"

"Why?" Carol said. "Is there something going on that shouldn't be?"

"No," he said. "Just kidding around. You know I do that sometimes." He glanced at Jodi and Harold curiously. "I'm Art Teal. You know, Teal like the bird. That's why I put a picture of a Teal on my advertising. Like the one on the sign outside the garage."

"Is that what that is?" Carol asked. "It looks more like a crow to me."

Teal's eyes narrowed, and Jodi got the sudden impression there was a great deal of animosity between him and the sergeant.

"Well, Art Teal like the bird," Carol said. "We have a warrant to get into Donna Esterhazy's apartment. We'd like the keys."

"Something happened to Donna?" he asked.

"The key," Carol insisted. "We'd hate to break the door down."

"No need for that," Art Teal said.

He padded inside and returned a moment later with a key.

"Donna in some kind of trouble?" Art Teal asked.

"Why?" Blankenship asked. "You a good friend of hers?"

"Not a close friend," he said. "I'm her landlord. I see her around. Cops show up with a warrant. I'm curious. It's only natural."

"Yeah," Blankenship said. "Natural. I think we'll be back to talk to you later. Don't go anywhere."

"I'll be either here or in my office next door," Teal said.

They left him and made their way to the other end up the complex and Donna's apartment. The inside of the apartment was a surprise. It was a lot more luxurious than the outside looked. It was wide and spacious. A large bay window let in a lot of light. The entry had polished hardwood and an oriental throw rug that looked expensive.

There was more hardwood in the living area with another expensive looking rug. The furniture was quality. It did not come from the local department store. An expensive looking oil original of a lake scene hung above a fake fireplace. Another oil painting hung on the far wall. The walls looked freshly painted.

"I thought it would be a dump from the outside," Carol said. "I wish my apartment was this classy inside."

"I'm taking the bedroom," Blankenship said. "You two do what you like."

"Is he always so charming?" Carol asked.

"I haven't known him long," Jodi said, "but I'm beginning to think he doesn't improve with time."

"So, what are we looking for?" Carol asked.

Jodi explained how Donna had been found dead on Carver Beach, and Blankenship was out to prove the Sandy Shoals mayor's son had killed her. Ugly politics were involved.

"Always," Carol said.

"I got the feeling you know Art Teal," Jodi said.

"Unfortunately," Carol said. "We suspect Mr. Teal doesn't just work on cars, but he also steals them. He's a slippery sod, but one day we will catch him."

"I take it you're not from around here," Jodi couldn't resist saying.

"I was actually born in the US," Carol said, grinning. "My parents were here on vacation, and I came along a little prematurely. They took me back to England where I lived for the first twenty-two years of my life, and now I can't seem to lose the accent."

"How did you end up working as a police officer in Savannah?" Jodi asked.

"It's a long story. I fell in love with an Air Force guy and he brought me back to the US. It was good for a while. Then it got bad. We divorced. He moved on. I stayed in Savannah. I like the area."

It still didn't explain how she had ended up a police officer, but perhaps she had followed the same path as Jodi. The job was available.

Carol took the kitchen and Jodi the front room. There was not much to search. The furniture appeared solidly made, heavy. Hard to move even slightly. Two end tables by the couch were both empty. A glass coffee table had a collection of magazines featuring design, art and photography.

"What did Donna do for a living?" Carol said, returning to the living room.

"We don't know anything about her," Jodi said. "We do suspect she worked for an escort service at one time in Athens."

"One thing for sure. She was not a chef. There was nothing much in the kitchen."

"But this place sure smells like money," Jodi said.

"You think maybe she was still in the same business?" Carol asked.

"I think it's a possibility," Jodi said.

"Let's switch," Carol said. "You take the kitchen. I'll look in here. Second pair of eyes."

The kitchen was out of Better Homes and Gardens, classic, neat, with all the shining and expensive gadgets. None of them looked used. A blender sat on one shelf still in the box with the price tag attached. There was a half-empty bottle of Chardonnay in the refrigerator, and a rotten apple on the counter. She dropped the apple into the trash and found Donna standing at her elbow. She almost gave a startled yelp but caught herself just in time.

It wouldn't do to have Blankenship and Carol come rushing in the kitchen to her sound of alarm.

"So, this is where I lived?" Donna said.

At least Donna was not quite as dead looking anymore. Easier to look at it. A little bit of her prettiness was shining through the crab bites. She still smelled of the sea, but not so overpowering. And she had changed her clothes. She wore a simple yellow sundress. No shoes. She looked younger, almost girlish.

"This was your apartment," Jodi said.

"I had a lot of nice things," she said.

"You sure did," Jodi said. "Maybe you could explain to me how you got all these nice things? Or what was your relationship to Billy? Or who killed you? Or anything?"

No answer, of course.

Jodi tried again. "What were you doing at Blackbeard's Tavern?"

Donna stamped her foot like a little girl having a temper tantrum. "Why are you asking me these questions. You're making my head hurt."

"I don't think anything can hurt you anymore," Jodi said.

"A lot you know," she said.

Jodi was left talking to empty air. The dead woman was right. She knew nothing, and she was finding out less every minute.

Jodi went back into the living area.

"It's weird," Carol said. "This room doesn't feel lived in. There's no spare change under the couch cushions, no stains. No personal photos. It's like a museum."

"She seemed very neat," Jodi said.

"Neat is one thing," Carol said. "But this goes way beyond neat. It's like somebody came in and cleaned the place."

"Nothing in the bedrooms," Blankenship said, as he returned. "I'm going to check the kitchen."

Jodi and Frances left the kitchen to him and went to check the bedrooms. The larger bedroom with the bath was not used as a bedroom. It had a wooden easel under the window and there were several canvases scattered around the room. The canvases were all landscapes. Jodi looked closer. On each a photograph was pinned to the left edge of the canvas and it looked as if the artist tried to copy the photograph.

The landscapes weren't very good.

"Struggling artist," Jodi said.

"I don't think she got a lot of money selling these," Carol said.

The bathroom had a huge tub and a small glass-enclosed shower. The medicine cabinet held only a couple of pill bottles.

"Aspirin and birth control," Frances said.

A toothbrush and toothpaste on the sink.

"Neat," Jodi said. "Neat and clean."

"I've always heard that clutter is a sign of a healthy mind," Carol said. "At least I hope so. This place definitely doesn't look as lived in as my apartment."

The other bedroom was just as neat. In the closet dresses were neatly hung on hangers, underwear carefully folded in dresser drawers. There were more expensive shoes, also neatly arranged in a plastic shoe rack.

It looked as if everything Donna wore was a designer item.

There was a single bed in the apartment, a large queen-sized covered with a beautiful silk comforter that looked Asian.

“Comforter’s worth more than my truck,” Carol commented.

"There’s something else odd,” Jodi said. “I know Billy was supposedly living here with her. But he hasn’t got the usual male stuff in the bathroom and none of his clothes are in the closet.”

“So, you’re thinking what?” Carol asked.

“I’m thinking someone did a good job of cleaning this place up. I just can’t figure out why.”

They found Blankenship in the front room.

"Nothing else to find here," he said. "I want to talk to that guy downstairs again. Teal, like the bird."

33.

Art Teal opened the door to their knock and led them into his kitchen. His apartment was a lot smaller than Donna's and a little cramped. Blankenship handed him a photograph of Billy Chutney.

"You ever see this guy with Donna?" Blankenship asked.

Teal studied the photograph for a moment and then nodded. "Yeah, I think I've seen him around sometimes."

"You ever hear his name?"

"No, he was never introduced. I think I heard her call him Buddy or Billy. Maybe Bill. Something like that."

"What did Donna do for a living?" Jodi asked. "That apartment she lived in looks expensive."

"It's not cheap," Art Teal said.

"So, how did she make her money?" Blankenship said. "You didn't rent her an apartment like that without knowing something about her finances."

"Of course not. I think she listed herself as an art student on her application. She had the down payment. She paid her rent on time. I didn't ask a lot of questions."

Blankenship kept asking questions in rapid-fire fashion and it appeared Teal was getting flustered, but it was obvious Blankenship wasn't after Teal. Blankenship had made up his mind that Billy Chutney was guilty. He was only fishing for more evidence against the mayor's son.

Jodi only half-listened to the answers to Blankenship's

questions. Her mind was on something else, something that she had noticed and discarded, and now was tugging at her consciousness again. Blankenship had put the black and white photograph on the table in front of Teal and trying not to be obvious, she pulled it a little closer.

The first time she saw it, she had only been concerned that it was Billy. Now she looked carefully at the background behind the couple. She recognized part of the sign and knew they were standing in front of the Sad Cow, but on the street just behind Donna was a dark colored Lexus.

"You think Donna was good looking?" Blankenship asked.

Art Teal looked uncomfortable. "Well, yeah, of course. She was good looking, but we didn't have anything going, if that's what you're getting at. We just spoke now and then."

"Nothing more?" Blankenship asked.

"Look, she was packaged well, and I admit I might have tried, except I've got a girl."

He glanced toward the back bedroom. Jodi thought she heard a noise from back there earlier. "Connie."

The girl who stepped out of the bedroom looked around nineteen. She walked to Teal's side and put a hand on his shoulder. Her eyes flickered nervously around. She was sort of skinny and not all that pretty, and it was hard to determine the real color of her hair because most of it was a bright orange. Jodi thought the best way to describe her would be fragile.

"Okay,' Blankenship said. "If we need to ask you anything else, will you be here?"

Teal visibly relaxed. "Always."

"What kind of car did Donna drive?" Jodi asked.

Blankenship hesitated, as if he realized it was a question he should have asked.

"Her car," Teal said, licking his lips. He was suddenly nervous. "Yeah, I think she had a Lexus."

"She didn't bring it to your garage for work?" Jodi asked.

He shook his head.

"That seems sort of odd," Jodi said. "I mean, you're so close and all. It seems like it would have been convenient for her to have your garage do her maintenance."

"No," he said. "I think she took it back to the dealer. A lot of cars, you do that to keep the warranty good."

It was obvious Teal was lying about something. He was already nervous, and he had gotten even more nervous when she mentioned the car.

But Blankenship was ready to go. He started out the door. Jodi would have liked staying around to find out what was bothering Teal. She felt there was more to learn, but she reluctantly got up and followed Blankenship outside. Teal slammed the door behind them.

"I don't think Teal was telling us everything he knew," Jodi said.

"He probably wasn't, "Blankenship said. "It doesn't matter. This picture proves Billy Chutney knew the woman, and more than likely killed her. I think the DA will bring charges."

Carol gave Jodi a look of sympathy as Blankenship hurried to his car and drove off.

"That guy is unbelievable," Carol said.

"Welcome to my world," Jodi said.

She had a late breakfast with Carol at a nearby Waffle House before heading back to Sandy Shoals. They got some strange looks from people as they entered. She knew it was the height thing. Carol was so petite, and she was so tall.

"Do you always eat like this?" Carol asked, a few minutes into breakfast.

"Only when I'm hungry," Jodi said.

"And I bet you're always hungry," Carol said.

Carol had coffee and a pastry, but Jodi finished off bacon and eggs and extra toast, orange juice and coffee. She felt a little better when she was finished.

"It took me a while, but I finally figured out where I had seen you before," Carol said. "The Dancing Girl."

"The video follows me around," Jodi said.

"And now you're Sandy Shoals chief of police," Carol said. "Have you hired anyone yet. I heard the rumor that everyone in the department was fired."

"The rumor is true," Jodi admitted. "Unfortunately, they kept one."

"He that bad?" Carol asked.

Jodi nodded. "And you know he has potential. He might have turned into a good police officer except he's full of macho and resents me having the job."

"I know the type," Carol said. "A woman's place is in the home."

"Exactly," Jodi said.

"You know, I originally put in my application in Sandy Shoals."

"Seriously?"

"I did. When I first divorced, I got an apartment near Carver Beach. I wanted to stay in that area. There were a couple of jobs available. One, as a waitress at the Seaside Café in the Springs area, and the other as a police officer. I put in applications to both."

"And what happened?"

"The police officer job was a joke. They already had hired someone, but I guess they feared the Government looking into their hiring practices or something. Chief Ballard wasn't even part of the interview process, and I discovered later that nobody was hired unless Ballard met with them. He had total control. Later, I got a phone call from a friend who told me I should try somewhere else because Ballard wasn't ever going to hire a woman."

"So, what did you do?"

"I tried the waitressing thing for a while. I hated it. Then my Mom sent me a long letter. It was kind of a I- told- you- so, letter. She wanted me to come back to England to live. I wasn't ready to do that. I saw the ad for Savannah police officers, and I decided to go for it. I ended up getting the job. Where Ballard wasn't hiring women, Savannah was trying to hire them."

"Why did you want to be a police officer," Jodi asked.

"Oh, I didn't mention it. I grew up at the local police station. Dad was a former SAS commando who went to work with the local police. I guess it felt natural."

Jodi finished the last bites of her toast and finished off her coffee.

"Are you ecstatically happy in Savannah?" Jodi asked.

Carol smiled. "Not ecstatically."

"There are positions open with the Sandy Shoals police department," Jodi said.

"What positions?" Carol asked.

"Everything except chief," Jodi said. “Although I’m thinking even that might be up for grabs.”

34.

The weatherman predicted it was going to stop raining soon, but it seemed to be coming down a little harder when Jodi left Sandy Shoals in Geoff's pickup truck. Geoff had looked at her a little odd when she asked if she could borrow it, but he didn't ask questions. He simply handed over the keys.

She would have explained if he asked. Doing any kind of surveillance work was kind of hard in a police car. People tended to notice. She knew she was probably breaking a half-dozen protocols she had been taught at the Georgia police academy. Nobody knew where she was going or what she was doing.

She might have told Geoff if he had asked but she was glad he hadn't.

She found a radio station out of Florida playing oldies from the sixties. She drove to Savannah listening to what she called her dad's music, classical rock from Elvis, Ricky and the Beatles.

The station played the rock song Momma Told Me Not To Come by Three Dog Night a couple of times.

She wondered if it was an omen.

The old cemetery had a massive gate with stone pillars, but the gate was open. She backed in the pickup truck so that she was hidden in trees. Rain beat on the top of the pickup and there was only a sliver of a moon. The truck was well-hidden, but she could see the front offices of the automotive shop. Next to the front office was a chain link fence that went around a wide area filled with cars. It went through her mind that it would be easy to hide a new Lexus in the yard.

"Why are we here?" Donna asked.

This time Donna had a real face, no crab bites. She wore a tight-fitting red dress, off the shoulder. A string of pearls around her neck. For the first time Jodi could see what Billy might have seen in her.

"We are watching the place where you used to live," Jodi said.

"Why?"

"I'm not sure why. It's something to do."

"That seems sort of stupid," Donna said.

"Surveillance is the true heart of police work," Jodi said.

"That sounds like something you made up," Donna said.

With the campus police, Jodi had participated in a few stakeouts, but always with other officers. She had never had a stakeout with ghost before.

"She's always been sort of flaky," Timothy said.

Timothy appeared next to the passenger side window and she now had two ghosts' sitting with her in the front seat of the pick-up. In a cemetery. Unbelievable. She didn't need to hunt for ghosts in spooky places. She brought her own.

"But sometimes she can be sort of intuitive about things," he said.

She closed her eyes. This was ridiculous. Her psychosis was out of control.

"Both of you go away," Jodi said.

"We'd still be married, and I'd still be alive if she wasn't so intuitive," Timothy said.

"That's not fair," Jodi said.

"She should have been in class," Timothy said, "but she got this feeling that I was in trouble and she came home unexpectedly. Then I really was in trouble."

Jodi hated thinking about it. Opening the door to her bedroom. Finding out how stupid she'd been. Wanting to run to her father, but realizing she was no longer talking to her father and ending up blaming him and Kate for her misery.

The thought struck her like a blow to her stomach.

Blaming her father and Kate for her own stupid decisions.

She still didn't like it, but she was starting to see things a little clearer.

Across the street, a car pulled up in front of the apartment building and sat idling for a few minutes. She tried to ignore her ghosts as the car door opened. The single light was not enough to illuminate much, and the rain created a haze. She could make out only a shadowy figure getting out. The figure went to Teal's front door and knocked. The door opened and the figure disappeared inside. A light came on in the area where the kitchen was.

She wondered if it was the girlfriend visiting.

She waited for a while longer and the front door opened. For a moment she could see the shadow of a woman in the dim light from the inside of Teal's apartment. The woman seemed taller than Teal's girlfriend. The door shut. The woman got into the car and drove away. A few minutes later another car pulled in, and the entire thing was repeated.

Another woman.

From where Jodi sat, she could not make out the license plate of the car, but she was curious. She opened the door and stepped out.

"What are you doing?" Timothy and Donna asked together.

"Exercising," she said. "Why don't you two get reacquainted. You used to know each other well."

She walked cautiously out of the cemetery and crossed the road. She knelt behind the car and used her cellphone to take pictures of the tag number.

What did detectives do without cellphones? Probably had to always carry a notebook and a pencil like the sergeant on the old television show, Dragnet.

Just the facts, Mam.

The rain seemed to come a little harder and she went to the corner of the building and stood. Standing there in the shadows, nobody would see if her unless she moved, and she could see the doorway.

Another few minutes passed, and it did open. A woman with lots of thick bond hair, and a short dress that looked painted on. Tottering on very high heels and a cloud of perfume. She walked to her car, got in, and drove away.

Jodi debated if she should stay where she was for a while, and even as she was thinking about it, another car pulled up in front. The headlights moved over, and she stopped herself from jumping back in alarm. It would have drawn attention.

Another woman. This time dressed like a schoolgirl with a plaid skirt and white blouse, her hair in pigtails. Part of her hair was orange. The door opened and a man stood framed in the doorway. Jodi gasped. Boris Petak could not be mistaken for anyone else. He reached for the girl's arm and pulled her into the room. The door slammed again.

What was Boris Petak doing in Art Teal's apartment?

Jodi stayed where she was, and the process was repeated by four other women in the next thirty minutes.

After the fourth woman left, Jodi hurried back to the pickup.

Her ghosts were gone.

She waited for another visitor, and when that women left and drove away, Jodi followed.

35.

It seemed like a long time, but the woman stopped at the same Waffle House where Jodi had eaten breakfast with Carol.

The breakfast crowd was gone. Only a few people were inside.

Three women sat at a large booth near the back. The oldest was a tough looking blond in her early forties. The harsh lights of the restaurant were unforgiving. Thick pancake makeup on her face could no longer hide the wrinkles. Her mascara was streaked. She wore a starched white nurse's uniform that fit like a second skin. She even wore the cap. Jodi was pretty sure nurses didn't wear the caps anymore. She was also pretty sure the woman wasn't a nurse.

The other two women were younger and prettier. One wore a simple black cocktail dress with stockings and high heels and pearls at her neck. Lots of cleavage. The other was the girl Teal had introduced as Connie. She wore the schoolgirl outfit with orange pigtails.

All three wore too much perfume, and the cloying scent became almost sickening as Jodi waked closer. They were all having coffee, orange juice, and breakfast platters piled high with eggs, bacon, grits and toast.

The blond was saying something that made the rest laugh, but conversation stopped as Jodi reached their table.

"I'd like to talk about Art Teal, like the bird," Jodi said.

Only Connie showed any sign of recognition.

"Or maybe we can talk about Donna Esterhazy, and who

murdered her."

Connie gasped. The other two women gave her a nasty look.

"I don't think we know anybody with those names, Red," the blond said. "Go away and leave us alone."

"We don't like to be bothered," the brunette said. "And we have friends who might take offense to your interrupting our meal. You wouldn't like to meet our friends."

"I don't think you'd like to meet my friends either," Jodi said.

"I think she's a cop," Connie said.

Timing was perfect because Sergeant Carol Grady chose that moment to walk into the restaurant in her uniform. Jodi had called her earlier. She smiled at Jodi and took a seat in a booth to the right of the three women.

"I never knew cops came in your size, Red," the blond said.

"You are sure a tall drink of water," the brunette said.

"Art Teal," Jodi said.

"We don't know him," the three of them said at once.

"That's strange," Jodi said. "Because he introduced Connie here as his girlfriend when I met him the first time. And I've just watched all three of you, plus several others, meeting at his apartment. I guess you were tallying weekly receipts. I know it's crass to talk about money, but how much do you girls take in every week? And what kind of percentage do you give Teal?"

"We don't know what you're talking about," the blond said.

"How much did Donna make?" Jodi asked. "I hope it was a lot. I hope it was worth having the life strangled out of her."

This time none of the women responded, but Connie looked a little pale.

"I don't care about your business," Jodi said. "I only want to find out who killed Donna."

Still, no response from any of them.

"I thought she was strangled by that kid," the blonde said.

"He wouldn't have hurt her," Connie blurted out.

Both the other women looked at her as if she had spoken treason.

"I met her mother," Jodi said. "A parent should never have to bury a child."

"We can't help you, Red," the brunette said. "Please go and let us finish our breakfast in peace."

"I still don't think the kid would have hurt her," Connie said. "They had feelings for each other."

The blond snorted.

"They did. And I liked Donna. She wanted to be an artist."

"Shut up, Connie," the blond said.

"She showed me some of her pictures," Connie said. "She was only going to work a couple more years. Then she was going to go to Paris and study art."

"Will you shut up," the blond said harshly. "I can't enjoy my breakfast. You're making me ill. Let's get out of here."

She looked aggressively at Carol as if she expected Carol to stop her. Carol only shrugged and grinned.

"Leave money for your breakfast," Carol warned. "You wouldn't want to be arrested for theft by taking."

The blond slapped down a ten-dollar bill on the table. The brunette did the same as she followed the blond. They both hesitated, waiting on Connie but Connie didn't move. The young woman looked tired and fragile, and almost near tears.

Jodi slipped into the booth beside her, mostly to prevent her from leaving. The cloying smell of perfume remained. The piles of eggs and bacon hadn't been touched but probably for the first time in her life, Jodi had no appetite.

"You were leaving," Carol said to the other two.

The blond gave Connie a nasty look and said. “Just watch what you say."

"Is that some kind of threat?" Jodi asked.

The blond didn't answer as she turned abruptly and left.

"Kind of a scary woman," Carol said.

Connie shrugged.

"I suspect she’s not really a nurse,” Carol said.

"No," Connie said. "Some guys like the cosplay thing."

Carol nodded. “As I always suspected. A lot of men are just weird.”

Connie started to pick at her own breakfast.

"Tell me about Professor Timothy Maxwell," Jodi asked.

"Connie looked puzzled. "Timothy? Why do you want to know about Tim? He didn't hurt Donna. He died."

"I know," Jodi said. "I'm just guessing but I'm betting that you knew him. I know Donna did."

"I knew him," Connie said. "I thought he was so distinguished and good looking, and smart. He was a professor."

"I know," Jodi said. "How did you meet him?"

"Donna introduced me. I just started school, and I met Donna at the gym. The professor picked her up that day."

"Donna was dating him?" Jodi asked.

"Yes. She knew he was married but he told her he was going to divorce his wife. We hung around together sometimes, but then he started making me nervous. You know how some men are. They hug you a little longer than they should. A hand touches a shoulder or arm and lingers."

"He flirted with you while he dated Donna," Jodi said.

"Yes."

"Then somehow she wasn't with him anymore and she started hanging around with the two brothers that owned the Sad Cow Restaurant. She said she and the professor weren't seeing each other anymore, but they were still friends. I didn't see any harm when he called and asked me out."

"But then the professor eventually introduced you to Boris Petak?" Jodi asked.

"Yes," Connie said miserably. "Him and his brother."

Connie stopped trying to pick at her food. She pushed her plate away.

"But why did you go along with it?" Carol asked. "Surely, you knew what you were getting into."

"I don't know why," Connie said. "It's just the professor talked me into doing things, and after a while I just didn't seem to have any self-respect anymore."

From the terrible pain evident in Connie's yes, Jodi could imagine the kinds of things Timothy had demanded, things that he had hinted around in their time together. Starting with the tattoo.

Jodi was pretty sure if her ex-husband wasn't already dead, she might have killed him herself.

"Could this professor have drugged you?" Carol asked. "Put something in your drink or food?"

"I suppose so," Connie answered.

Jodi gave her an inquiring look.

"There are mixtures of drugs," Carol said. "Given over a period of time, they can wear somebody's resistance down, make them more pliable."

It was something Jodi hadn't considered up until then, but it made a kind of sense. Timothy was charming but he wasn't so charming to account for all the success he had with the coeds on campus.

She wondered if Timothy had used any of those drugs on her.

She shivered. She felt suddenly very cold all over.

"Donna got so angry," Connie said.

"Angry?" Jodi asked. "Why?"

"Donna didn't know I was with the professor until he brought me to one of the parties," Connie said. "I never saw her so mad as she was when she saw us together. I thought it was jealousy, but it was something else. Maybe she felt guilt for ever introducing us. I guess it's good he had the heart attack."

"Why?"

"Because Donna might have done something drastic," Connie said. "Her, and that weird sister of hers."

A momentary image went through her mind. Cat Esterhazy surrounded by herbals remedies, exotic concoctions. She wondered if any of those could cause congestive heart failure in a healthy middle-aged man. Maybe Donna had gotten her revenge with her sister's help. If the coroner had missed it, it was unprovable now. Cremation had forever hidden any evidence.

Cat Esterhazy had claimed she didn't know who Donna's professor was, but Jodi was pretty sure she was lying.

Her dead ex-husband suddenly appeared in the booth next to Carol, but he didn't look as sharply defined as usual. He looked a little transparent, like Donna when she had first started appearing. There were a few holes showing through.

"I knew my heart was in good shape," he said indignantly.

She was tempted to shout that his heart was black as coal. She closed her eyes for a moment, but he was still there when she opened them again. He shimmered in soft light of the restaurant. He looked a little more like ghosts were supposed to appear. Maybe her psychosis was finally catching up to reality.

"I was murdered," Timothy said. "That little witch killed me."

"You don't know that for sure," Jodi said.

"What?" Carol asked. "What don't I know for sure?"

"Sorry," Jodi said quickly. "I was just thinking out loud."

She turned her head so she couldn't see Timothy.

"And now you are working for Boris Petak?" Jodi asked. "I saw him. At Art Teal's place. I know he had an escort service in Athens. And now he's running one in Savannah. Or is Art Teal running it for him?"

Connie looked as if she was having second thoughts about saying anything more, but Carol moved so that she was across the booth from her and she reached and took both Connie's hands in her own. For a small woman, Carol's physical presence seemed to fill the booth.

"Listen to me, Connie," Carol said. "I know you're unhappy. I can see it in your face. You don't want to spend your life doing what you're doing. I can help you. We want to help you. But you have to tell us what's going on."

Connie shook her head. "He'll hurt me."

"You mean Teal?"

"Yes."

"Like he hurt Donna?" Jodi asked.

Connie shook her head more violently. "He wouldn't hurt Donna. He loved Donna. It wasn't like it was with the rest of us. Donna was special to him."

Jodi began to have a glimmer of understanding. "Art Teal loved Donna. But so did Billy. What would Art have done if he found out Donna was going to leave him and marry Billy?"

Connie's pale face was the answer.

36.

For the second time that evening, Jodi found herself in front of Donna's apartment building, but this time without her ghosts. She was with Carol and two burly Savannah police detectives. Connie sat beside Jodi in the back seat. She had already given them enough information to get a warrant. It was as if she had been waiting on someone to ask her the questions, and she couldn't stop talking. Jodi thought down deep Connie had been hurting for a long time, wanting to find some way out of her life.

The amount of information surprised even the cynical detectives. Art Teal had evidently thought she couldn't see, hear, or understanding anything. He had talked freely around her. He had even had her type up some of his business expenses.

Connie knew there was a logbook in the safe that had transactions that didn't go on his tax returns.

She knew about the stolen cars.

And she knew that he rented apartments to his escorts.

"There is one thing I still don't understand," Jodi asked. "How does Art Teal fit in with Boris Petak? Is he a friend of the family? What?"

Connie looked confused at the question. "Bede, of course."

"You mean Boris Petak's brother? He has something to do with this. I thought he moved to Oregon or somewhere?"

She shook her head. "He only went there to get his name changed. He thought it was funny."

"What was funny?"

"The name he chose. Teal. Petak means bird in Polish."

Art Teal, like the bird.

Bede Petak.

Savannah police detectives showed up with warrants and they went in just a couple of hours before daylight. The warrants specifically covered both Art Teal's apartment and his place of business. Other officers entered the garage as they knocked on Teal's apartment door.

Nobody answered their knock and the two detectives broke the door open with a few savage kicks. Inside the apartment felt cold, deserted.

"Art Teal has run," Carol said.

In the kitchen a chair was knocked over and in the back bedroom a safe was open, but half the contents were still inside. Teal and his brother Boris had left in a hurry.

"One of those women at the Waffle House warned them Connie was talking," Carol said.

But they had left a lot of stuff behind in their haste. The logbook Connie had mentioned was gone but there were piles of paper left behind.

One of the detectives made a slow circular motion with his finger when he read the top paper.

"Numbers of credit cards. I bet we find they are stolen. A lot of receipts. You said this Boris Petak ran a restaurant?"

"Yes," Jodi answered. "The Sad Cow in Athens."

"Exactly where a lot of these receipts are from," the detective said. "We'll contact the Athens police, but I believe they are running some kind of credit card identity theft and it could be enough to put these guys away for a while."

Underneath the bed there was a box of photographs. Jodi

looked at one, and it was enough. They were not art.

"Names and dates on the back," Carol said. "Interesting."

"Only if you're a voyeur," Jodi said.

"No, it was more than that. I recognized a couple of men in the pictures. Local politicians. Men with wives at home. Maybe he had a little blackmail thing going on?"

There was also a 38 caliber Smith and Wesson revolver. One of the detectives took it out to his car and ran the number. Stolen.

In the closet, Carol discovered a loose floorboard at a place where the carpet bunched up. Underneath were boxes of watches and rings, and several more guns. More photos.

"I'm thinking escort service, blackmail, burglary, and car theft."

"The brothers believed in capitalism," Jodi said.

The detectives couldn't be happier with what they had found, and they were even happier when they found the other officers had discovered a half-dozen stolen cars in the fenced-in area. They had already found the missing logbook.

There was enough to lock the Petak brothers up for a long time, but nothing that would prove Billy Chutney innocent.

They found the Lexus covered with a heavy blue tarp in the far corner of the fenced-in yard.

"Do you think we could get your evidence team to go over it?" Jodi asked Carol. "I'm not sure our sheriff's guys would do their upmost to find evidence clearing Billy. Hopefully, there could be fingerprints or blood or something of Art Teal's in the car. I'd like to prove that he drove it last."

"Because it would mean he drove it back from Carver Beach," Carol said.

"Yes. I know Billy and Donna had the car at Carver Beach, and if we could prove Art Teal drove it last, it would prove he was at Blackbeard's Tavern."

"I'll have it hauled to the evidence compound and our guys will go over it carefully," Carol said. "We've been trying to catch Art Teal in something for several years. I think right now you could ask for anything you like, and you'd get it."

"I still have those job openings," Jodi reminded her.

"I'll think about it," Carol said, "but you know this is also great for me. I could make lieutenant out of this."

"Hoisted on my own petard," Jodi said.

37.

She felt weary down deep.

It seemed as if she had been tired ever since she had arrived in Sandy Shoals.

But things were looking a little better for Billy Chutney. Surely Teal's fingerprints (she still wasn't thinking of him as a Petak) would be on the car and it being in his parking lot should prove that someone, if not him, had driven it back from Carver Beach. It proved someone else had been at Blackbeard's Tavern.

She had to stop for coffee at another Waffle House along 17, and back in the old truck, she turned the radio up loud, hoping the coffee and the music would keep her alert.

Immediately the music was interrupted by a news report. She heard her own name mentioned several times as the broadcaster gave an account of the raid on Teal's garage. It sounded like someone on her side had written the report. She stayed in the Waffle House parking lot listening to the report and getting the information that Boris Petak had been arrested while trying to leave from the Savannah airport and was now being questioned by the police. Bede Petak (aka Art Teal) was still at large.

She took a sip of coffee as her ex-husband appeared in the seat next to her. He was even more transparent than he had appeared in the restaurant and there were large holes in parts of him as if someone had fired a full load of buckshot into his form.

"You're looking a little pale," Jodi commented.

"Not funny," he said. "Do you think that crazy witch really murdered me? You think she gave me something to make me have a heart attack?"

"I don't know," Jodi admitted.

"You don't seem to be concerned about it," he accused her.

"Honestly. I'm not. What happened to you is not at the top of my priority list."

"You care more about that kid being arrested," he said. "I was your husband."

Jodi shook her head. "Yes. But you were never very good at that."

"You only married me to make your daddy mad. Because he married your friend."

"Yes," Jodi admitted. She sipped her coffee. "That's right. I know that now. And you know something else? I just realized something. I'm not mad anymore. I want my life back. I want to go out on the Gypsy with Kate, and I want to laugh with her again."

"And what about me?"

"Why should I care about you? You were seducing young girls and then turning them over to a pimp. You're disgusting."

"Maybe if you had been more loving?"

Jodi sighed. "Carol was right. Men are just weird."

"You never understood me," he said.

"You are just beyond belief," she said. "You didn't murder Donna Esterhazy, but you caused her death. Worse, you killed the souls of a lot of other young girls. I'll never know how many. And what if Cat Esterhazy did kill you? If she did, she probably saved my life. If I had discovered what kind of monster you were, I might have murdered you myself."

"You don't mean that," he said

She got out of the truck and walked a few feet away. There wasn't much traffic. A single car passed on the road, headlights glistening in the rain. She sipped her coffee. She wasn't only tired. She was mad. She had never felt so angry. She had meant what she said. At that moment, if he wasn't already dead, she would have killed him.

Which was kind of sick because she was still sure he only existed in her mind.

"I'm feeling kind of sick," Timothy said.

"You can't be sick," she said. "You're dead."

"No, I'm sick," he said.

He was glowing. Not like a light. Kind of like those tiny silver fish sometimes seen just underneath the surface of the sea. Shimmering, Ghostly.

And he wasn't dressed.

He wasn't naked. It was hard to explain. His body had no clothes, but it wasn't formed. Parts of him were not even there. By the second, he was becoming less.

"I think you're finally leaving me," Jodi said.

"I don't like this much," he said.

"I always knew," she said. "You were too young to die. You took care of yourself. You wouldn't even take an aspirin when you had a headache. A heart attack didn't make sense."

"The witch killed me," he said.

"I still don't know that for sure," Jodi said. "But yes, it's possible."

"You're going to arrest her," he said.

"It's doubtful. You wanted to be cremated. The coroner says it was a heart attack. Your ashes were scattered. It would be very hard to prove."

"You don't want to prove it," he accused her.

Jodi thought about it a moment. "You know, I don't know

what it says about me, but I think you're right."

"You never loved me," he said.

"And you never loved anybody but yourself," she said.

He was gone. No glowing light. No dead ex-husband. She was alone in the dark in the parking lot of a dimly lit Waffle House. Talking to herself.

Probably she had always been talking to herself.

38.

Sometime later she stopped at a Plaza truck stop and got a fried egg sandwich and more coffee. She ate it in the truck. The sun was just beginning to come up as she drove into Sandy Shoals. She parked in the back and went through to find Frances San standing behind the reception counter.

"Hail the conquering hero," Frances said.

"What?"

"You are all over television this morning. News out of Brunswick and Savannah. Even the morning news out of Atlanta. They're showing the clip again."

"Oh, great," Jodi said.

"And they're also talking about how the new police chief of Sandy Shoals broke up a theft and prostitution ring, and how the mayor of Savannah is thinking of giving you the key to the city."

"Seriously?"

"And the county district attorney is making noises that sound like he's backing away from the prosecution of Billy Chutney now. Something about a car being found. They wanted to interview the sheriff, but he let them interview Harold Blankenship instead. Blankenship didn't have much to say."

"I bet," Jodi said.

"Right now, you could ask for an increase to your budget and you'd get it," Frances said.

"Right now, what I need is a nap."

"Stretch out on the couch in your office," Frances said.

"I don't have a couch in my office," Jodi said.

"Sure, you do," Frances said.

And she did. A comfortable looking couch and two chairs that matched, along with a new desk and chair that rolled. The plywood chair was gone. The windows had been cleaned and she had a view of the rear parking lot and the courthouse across the street. The once closed closet door was open and several uniforms hung on wooden hangars, still covered in plastic.

The bathroom had been cleaned and scrubbed, the adult magazines and the booze gone from the cabinets. A fragrance cannister with the hint of lemon was on top of the cabinet.

Even the shower stall had been scrubbed.

The place no longer smelled as strongly of stale cigarette smoke, but the odors still lingered. It would take time. Just like her car.

Jodi took Frances's advice. She stretched out on the couch and closed her eyes. It felt like only five minutes before Frances was shaking her.

"You'd better rise and shine," Frances said. "Geoff called. The DA has announced he will not be charging anyone with a crime yet. Billy can go home. The mayor and Sunni are ecstatic. From what I understand, the Sheriff is furious and there's talk Harold Blankenship may be transferred back to patrol on the midnight shift,"

"All this happened while I was asleep?"

"Evidently Savannah's crime scene unit found Donna Esterhazy's purse in the floor of her Lexus. There was blood on it. Hers. But there was also a fingerprint in the blood that belonged to Bede Petak."

"He didn't even take the purse out of the car," Jodi said.

"The height of arrogance," Frances said.

"I'm not sure," Jodi said. "I'm beginning to think it was the classic love triangle. Art Teal was in love with Donna, and Billy was in love with Donna. I don't know if Donna loved either of them, but I do know she saw in Billy an opportunity to change her life. Perhaps become the great artist she thought she could be. But I also think Teal/Petak was giving her money, and he thought that made her exclusive to him. I think he followed them out to Carver Beach. There was an argument. He hit Billy and then strangled Donna and then dropped her into the ocean. But I think he was messed up after he killed her. I think he might have been sorry."

"Maybe. But I sure don't want to ever be loved that way. How did he get out to Carver Beach if he drove her car back?"

Jodi shook her head. "We may never know that. The car he drove out there is probably at the bottom of the ocean somewhere. Maybe next to mine. Maybe when they find Petak, we'll have more answers."

"He's being looked for all over the state," Frances said. "He's very popular right now. I didn't mention it earlier but one of the stolen revolvers you found in his apartment came back as belonging to a police officer who was badly injured in a traffic accident while responding to a call. Somebody stopped, but instead of stopping to help, they stole his pistol and a shotgun. Then took off. Fortunately, the officer lived but a lot of people know the story. Bede Petak is not a popular citizen now, and I guarantee you he's being looked for diligently."

"Good," Jodi said.

"On to more normal stuff," Frances said. "We have several interviews set up on Monday. They all look good on paper. They scored high. But one never knows."

"Hopefully, they will all be new hires," Jodi said.

"And your new uniforms are here," Frances said.

"I don't remember ordering any," Jodi said.

"I did, for you. Because I wanted you to look nice in the pictures."

"What pictures?" Jodi asked suspiciously.

Frances glanced at her watch. "The ones you are going to be in about an hour from now. At the courthouse where you will be given a nice reception and you will be officially sworn in. The mayor's office will probably be packed. Everybody's interested in meeting the new police chief. I'm not sure if they want to meet The Dancing Girl or the state's new hero crime buster. It'll mean even more publicity. I think you've managed to put the sheriff's attempts to take over the city police on the back burner. Maybe for good."

Jodi took a long, hot shower and dressed in one of the new uniforms Frances had provided. How Frances had managed to get her measurements, she didn't know, but the uniforms fit perfectly. So did the highly polished uniform shoes. There was also a new uniform web belt with an empty holster. She left it in the closet.

It was still raining as she and Frances hurried across the street and up the steps to the courthouse. For the first time, there was a young woman behind the front reception desk.

"I'm Peggy Hamilton," she said, with a smile. "Everybody's in the mayor's office, Chief."

Another Hamilton. Sandy Shoals was full of them.

Even though Frances had warned her, she had not expected the crowd of people crammed into the mayor's office. All the city council was there, including Dr. Theo. Champagne was being served in plastic champagne glasses from a table Eunice had set up in a corner. It was surprising considering Sunni Chutney's temperance beliefs. Also, coffee. Jodi headed for the coffee, but she was intercepted by the mayor and Sunni.

"We both want you to know we appreciate the help you've been for Billy," Sunni said.

It looked a little like she really meant it, and there was honest gratefulness in her eyes.

She didn't feel like bursting their bubble of happiness but saying that Billy wasn't exonerated yet. There was still a lot of things that needed to be straightened out.

Geoff rescued her, grabbing her arm and pulling her away. He led her over to the coffee pot and she filled a Styrofoam cup. She had time for only a few sips before the owner, chief reporter, and photographer of the Sandy Shoals Gazette wanted pictures. She stood with Frances with their back against the back wall, where the city emblem and the “friendly city by the sea” was plainly visible.

"When everything settles down," Geoff said. "I'd like to have dinner with you. There's an Italian place in Savannah I've been wanting to try."

"Are you asking me out?" Jodi asked.

"I thought that was what I was doing," Geoff said.

"Then the answer is yes," Jodi said. "It's pretty hard to find someone to go out with who is taller than I am."

"That's your only reason?" Geoff asked.

"Maybe," she said teasingly.

For some reason she found herself looking over his shoulder and finding the eyes of Dr. Theo. Dr. Theo was smiling, a strange kind of smile.

Almost Machiavellian.

At least twenty pictures were made, several of her shaking the Mayor's hand, a couple with Geoff. Even some with Sunni.

The swearing in ceremony was short and sweet and more pictures were taken. For the first time, she felt like she was the police chief.

When she and Frances returned to the police station, she

found her father waiting on her. She hugged him. It felt right.

She walked her dad into her office, and he settled into one of her new chairs. Jodi sat on the couch.

"Why do I feel like I might be getting a lecture?" Jodi said.

"Did I lecture you all that much?" he asked.

"I always had trouble being the lady you thought I should be," Jodi said.

"But I was always proud of you," he said. "Never more so, than now."

Jodi shrugged. "I've got the job. Let's see how long I can keep it."

Her father nodded. "Kate wanted to come."

"I believe you," Jodi said. "What is it that you're having trouble saying?"

"I just don't want you to take it wrong," he said. "I want to know if everything is all right. Kate has been a new person lately. She's smiling again. It's like the old Kate is back. I wasn't sure she would ever be back after we lost the baby."

"And you're worried I might cause her to have a setback," Jodi said, understanding. "You think I might turn back into that angry, awful witch again."

"I'm just concerned," he said. "You were so angry for so long."

"Not anymore," she said.

He studied her face a moment, and then he nodded.

"Something has happened. I don't see the anger."

"Nope. Let's say I've put aside the ghost of the past. Kate and I will never always get along, but we didn't always get along before you married her. But she's my best friend. For a while I admit, I thought I hated her. I didn't. It's hard to explain. I had a terrible emptiness. I thought I had lost a friend. Two friends. You and her. I only wanted to strike back, to hurt you both as much as I thought you'd hurt me."

"We didn't want to hurt you, Jodi," he said. "I guess we could have managed telling you better. But then it was also a surprise to us. We never expected to develop feelings for each other. Not those kinds of feelings. We certainly never expected you to jump and marry that professor."

"Not my brightest moment," Jodi admitted.

"Are you still planning on going out on the Gypsy?" he asked.

"Just as soon as I can," Jodi said. "I'm looking forward to it. I told Kate I would come by on Saturday and we'd start getting her ready to go out."

"Going dancing on the waves," her father said.

"There is one thing, though. You might tell her."

"What?"

"I will never, ever, ever call her Mother."

39.

She spent the weekend at the marina with Kate and her father.

She slept on a cot in her old room and spent two days getting the Gypsy back in order. Her dad always insisted that they never cut corners.

"Always prepare to stay out a lot longer than you intended," was his mantra, and then he would start humming the theme to the old television show Gilligan's Island. He could be very annoying.

But every line was checked, and frayed ones replaced. Safety equipment and first aid kits were replenished. The main sail was in good shape, but the jib halyard had to be replaced, and new paint was applied liberally to everything. Because most of the yard's supplies had been swept away with the storm, Jodi ended up making several trips to the nearest boating store.

The Gypsy had a GPS system and a VHF radio. Her father also insisted on a handheld backup radio that was stored in the emergency kit. The boat even had a laptop to help with navigation.

The Gypsy had a Volvo gasoline engine that was old, but her father kept it in good shape. The day before they sailed, her father would make sure the batteries were all charged.

It was hard work and most of it was done by her and Kate.

In the evenings they all watched old movies and ate buttered popcorn and got to know each other again.

It was a good weekend and Monday morning Jodi showed up at work, showered, fed, and fully charged. Frances San was working in the back room with two temps and handed Jodi the file of people to be interviewed.

She would have preferred having help with the interviews, but it was all on her. There was only one other officer, and she wasn't about to include Hollis Bushnell. It was hard enough just keeping him doing his job.

She decided to change into another of the crisp new uniforms which she felt made everything more formal. She even felt a little optimistic as she waited the first officer-candidate. Five interviews later, she felt tired, discouraged and hungry. Out of five, there was not one viable candidate. One of them even smelled of alcohol.

"I'm going to get a sandwich," she told Frances, as she passed.

"Anyone yet?"

Jodi shook her head.

There were four more interviews in the afternoon and the second group seemed even worse than the first. At this rate she would never hire a soul.

She had her head back, her eyes closed, and she was feeling the pressure of the sea underneath the Gypsy, when someone cleared their throat. She opened her eyes and straightened up in her chair, and found Carol Grady standing in her doorway.

"Sleeping on the job, Chief?" Carol said.

"It's not been a good day," she said.

"No good applicants?" Carol said.

"Not a single one," she said.

"Then maybe I can help," Carol said.

Carol sat in the chair across from the desk and took out a couple of typewritten sheets from her purse. The two sheets contained nearly forty names and phone numbers. Out beside the name was also their current rank and the police department they worked with. A dozen were with Savannah but there were names from nearly every department around the state, even Atlanta PD.

"Of course, I don't know all of these guys personally," Carol said. "But they've all got clean records and they've all expressed an interest in transferring to another department."

"Malcontents," Jodi suggested.

"A few, probably. But it's a prospect list. More than we've got now."

"You said 'we've' got," Jodi said.

"I've decided to take your job offer," Carol said. "I've never worked for a woman. It could be interesting. And I think you're lucky."

"Lucky?'" Jodi said. "I don't understand."

"In one night, you broke up the biggest car theft ring in Savannah, not to mention an escort service, and all the other crimes involved. Who knows what the future will hold?"

"Public relations, I hope," Jodi said.

40.

It was dark when she left the police department. She had started bringing a jogging suit every day and jogging back to her apartment.

She was feeling a little better about everything.

The next day was Saturday and she and Kate were finally taking the Gypsy out. They had been working hard on her for three weekends in a row. Also, she was making progress on hiring. Carol had already been hired and was starting the following Monday. Carol would be the first watch supervisor hired. The rank of captain. Jodi had offered her the title of assistant chief, but Carol had turned it down.

"Paperwork enough with head of watch," Carol said.

At least she would have someone else to keep an eye on the elusive Hollis Bushnell.

Seven more from Carol's list were in the process of being hired, and an ad in the paper had brought in a rush of new, young and capable candidates.

The only thing that still troubled her was Billy Chutney. He was free, walking around, and there was doubt he would be charged with Donna Esterhazy's murder. But there was still lingering doubt in Jodi's mind. Perhaps she had played the political game a little too well, and she had allowed a murderer to go free.

She stopped to stretch before she began her run. She heard the snapping of a twig somewhere and she looked around. The darkness was causing strange shadows in the trees. She felt a presence and started to turn but then she felt something hard stab painfully into the small of her back.

"Are you armed?" a guttural voice asked.

"No," she said.

"Then let's go back to your car. You're taking me out of here."

She had no doubt who it was. She had located Bede Petak/ Art Teal. She caught a glimpse of his weapon as she turned to walk slowly back to her car. It was small. Perhaps a twenty-two, but even a twenty-two could do irreparable damage if fired against her spine.

He sounded a little raspy. His hand trembled. She had once been taught a technique where she could turn and disable an assailant if you could feel the pressure of the gun. It was kind of tricky, but it was fun to practice with a fake gun. It wasn't any fun when it was a real gun.

She decided not to risk it. She stopped at her car.

"You messed everything up," he said.

"No," she told him. "You did that when you killed Donna."

She waited for him to protest, but he didn't speak.

"I'm hungry," she said. "I bet you are too. Let's go someplace and get supper. Maybe ribs. There's this great rib place out on the highway."

"Shut up," he said.

"Okay," Jodi said. "You don't like ribs. How about fish? Blackbeard's Tavern has great fish. Or maybe you don't want to go back there anymore?"

He poked her with the pistol. It hurt.

"Will you shut up."

She stopped talking.

"They're looking for me all over," he said. "You're going to get me out of here.

"Oh," Jodi said. "How shall I do that? And you do know that kidnapping a police officer is a very bad idea."

"I know all about you," he said. "The Dancing Girl. The Professor used to talk about you a lot. I wanted him to bring you around. Introduce you. But then he married you. I never understood that."

"It confuses me a little too," Jodi said. "I try not to think about it."

"He said you can also handle a boat. Your dad has boats. You could get me out of the country on a boat."

"Seriously," Jodi said. "That's your plan? What country? You left all your passports in that box under the bed with your gun and all those dirty pictures. How are you supposed to stay in any country without a passport? Even if I could get you there. Which I can't because finding a boat provisioned and equipped to get you out of the country would take some time, and you don't have that much time."

"I'm not going to jail," he said.

"I think you should have thought of that a long time ago," Jodi said.

"No jail. It's your fault. You're going to help me. Maybe you can't get me out of the country, but you can get me out of Georgia. I read where you used to sail to Florida. You can take me there. I've got friends there."

"And why would I want to do that?" Jodi said.

"Because I'll shoot you if you don't," he said.

Jodi believed him. It was true. She had made the trip to Florida a half dozen times. It was a trip she could make with her eyes closed. But it also occurred to her that once he got her there, she wouldn't be of any use to him anymore. "Get in the car," he said. "You're driving. Nobody's going to stop a police car."

She got under the wheel. Bede Petak walked around and

opened the passenger side. She got her real good look at him. He looked as tired as she felt. He was soaking wet. A long scrape along his cheek showed dried blood.

"You drive carefully," he said.

"I always do," she said. "Especially when somebody threatens me with a gun."

She started the car and drove out of the parking lot. All the lights of Sandy Shoals were still not on. The town was still recovering. Captain Hook's Theater was dark and abandoned looking. In the summertime it was open five nights a week featuring shows with local talent. Jodi had auditioned for a few of the shows, but she was also so tall that she towered above everyone on stage.

There was a bar and restaurant next door, the Bounty. It was open but there were few customers.

Everything seemed very still as she drove out of Sandy Shoals and made the turn-off onto Highway 17 heading for the Marina. Time moved slowly. She shivered but she wasn't cold.

"It was an accident," Bede Petak/Art Teal said.

"Seriously?"

"I didn't mean to kill her. She was just acting so stupid."

"She wanted to marry Billy?" Jodi asked.

"Yes. He was going to take her to Paris, and she was going to learn to pain from the great artists. It was sad. She wasn't a painter. She would have done better painting houses. She had no talent."

"So, you strangled her because she had no talent," Jodi said. "And then you dumped her over a cliff like so much garbage."

"I told you," he said. "It was an accident. I didn't mean to kill her."

Jodi breathed an audible sigh of relief. Up until that moment, she wasn't sure. Billy still could have been guilty. It was another of those heavy burdens she had been carrying around, and now she was glad to let it go.

"So, what happened that night?" Jodi asked.

For a moment she was afraid he wasn't going to answer, but then he started to talk. His voice had gotten high like a small boy, and it quivered when he spoke.

"I did love her," he said. "I would have married her. Donna was different. She wasn't like the others. I told her that I'd take her to Paris. Or anywhere she wanted to go. I let her get away with a lot. She stopped working. I let that kid move into her apartment. My brother told me I was an idiot. Maybe I was."

"I can testify to the fact that love makes us do strange things sometimes," Jodi said.

"Yeah, sure," he said. "She started driving that kid all around town, visiting museums and stuff. They were inseparable. I kept trying to make her see that it wasn't going to work. He wasn't going to marry her. Then the night of the storm. She wanted to take photographs so she could paint it later. She thought a painting of the storm would be her masterpiece."

He grew quiet, looking out at the passing scenery but the gun remained pointed at her.

"You followed them that night?"

"Yeah. But I wasn't going to confront them. I had another idea. I had read about the kid. I knew all about his father getting elected mayor. And Donna told me about the kid's mother being such a witch. I was going to somehow get his parents out to the beach and let them confront the kid and Donna. I knew the kid was terrified of his mother. I figured that would break them up."

"But your plan didn't work?"

"The parents weren't in town. Then the storm came up too quick. I was worried about them. I headed out to the beach.

I found her bent over the kid. He was unconscious. He was bloody. Evidently a big board off one of the buildings had hit him in the head. We pulled the kid in her car and drove up to the first place we saw. The tavern. I broke in and we dragged the kid inside. I figured it was a good place to ride the storm out. We had a few drinks."

"Billy's clothes were soaked in alcohol," Jodi pointed out. "He smelled like a brewery."

"I poured a few bottles on him," he admitted. "I thought it was funny. She didn't. She scratched my face. The silly witch scratched me."

"And you strangled her," Jodi said.

"I was just trying to keep her from scratching me," he said.

Jodi finally had the entire story. Everything finally made sense. Except she was sitting in the car with a man and a gun, and she wasn't going to be able to tell anyone anytime soon.

"I loved her," Bede Petak said softly.

41.

All the way to the marina she kept thinking of things she might do. Each idea seemed more foolish or dangerous than the last.

“Why did you clean up her apartment?” Jodi asked. “I know it was you. You drove the Lexus back from the beach and then you cleaned out all of Billy’s clothes. You scrubbed the apartment down.”

“I just wanted him gone,” Petak said.

“I see,” Jodi said. “You thought you’d keep the apartment as your shrine to her.”

He didn’t answer, but Jodi thought it answered her last question. And proved what Carol said was right.

Some men were just strange.

There were few lights on at the marina. She parked near the granite slab. He told to step out and then he followed her out the driver's side.

"Find a boat," he said.

Of course, she would take the Gypsy and it was best if she took it quickly. Before her dad or Kate discovered them.

She led him along the dock. An idea came to her and she discarded it, and then it came back to her again. The dock was five foot wide. Bede was not very muscular looking. If he could be hit hard enough with the full force of her body, she was pretty sure he would end up in the water. All she needed was for him to come close enough again.

And a prayer for him being a bad shot.

Prod me again, she begged.

Just one more. Stick that gun in my back and I'll send you in the water.

Frustratingly, he wouldn't get close enough and then someone stepped out of the shadows in front of her.

Kate.

Oh no, she said.

"Both of you freeze," Bede shouted, like one of those cops on television. Except he wasn't a cop. He was a crazy man waving a gun around, and he was nearly as afraid as Jodi was. It went through her mind that the gun could go off by accident.

"Be still, Kate," Jodi said. "Just be still. Don't do anything."

Kate stood still.

"You turn around," he told Kate. "I want a boat. She's taking me to Florida. Now you're going along."

It was getting better and better.

Kate did as she was told. Jodi walked a few steps to her side. They both reached the Gypsy and Kate scrambled up the ladder. Jodi followed. Bede came more slowly, looking around, holding the gun out as if someone else might jump from the shadows. He was suddenly looking less sure of himself.

And as he stepped onto the deck, she noticed he limped a little.

“You hurt yourself?” she asked.

“Trick knee,” he said. “It bothers me sometimes.”

Jodi said a silent prayer of apology to Sunni Chutney. Freddie Thigpen was telling the truth about seeing a man with a limp.

"Okay, let's get this thing started," he said.

"Have you ever been on a small boat before?" Jodi asked.

"No," he said. "But I've been on plenty of cruises."

Jodi knew the feeling was very different on a sailboat, but she wasn't going to mention it.

"Will you get the lines, Kate?" Jodi asked.

"Stop," Bede said, waving his gun around. "What are you doing?"

"She's going to have to take the lines off," Jodi said patiently. "Or we'll never get away from the dock."

Mentally, she was hoping Kate would make the jump in the dark and take off in the darkness. Evidently Bede thought of the same thing because he pointed the gun at Jodi's head.

"You do anything but untie the lines and I'll shoot your friend," he threatened.

Jodi thought he would never get where he was going if he shot her, but she kept her opinion to herself.

It was a very quiet night, with an inky black darkness. There were only a few stars in the sky. Jodi turned on the running lights, started the engine, while Kate cast off the lines.

"Wait," Bede said. "How do I know you can do this in the dark?"

Jodi almost laughed. "You know, it's a bit late to ask me that. We have a compass. I'll find my way. I've done it lots of times. Easy."

He still looked suspicious, but he had little choice. He looked nervously around.

"How do you make this thing go?" he asked.

"It's a sailboat," Jodi said. "We sail."

Kate looked at her oddly, but Jodi made no attempt to turn on the engines. She prayed there was enough wind to get them away from the dock. Usually, she used the engines to get out and then went to the sails.

"Where are we going?" Kate asked.

"Saint Augustine," Jodi said. "You remember we went to Saint Augustine once. That was the time you fell in the water."

"I remember," Kate said, and she nodded as she understood what Jodi was getting at. She moved over to the other side of the boat and gripped the rails tight. It was going to be a rough ride.

"You know if it was really an accident," Jodi said. "You should turn yourself in. Get a good lawyer."

"Shut up," he said.

"I know a good lawyer," Jodi said. "I bet he'd be willing to take your case. He's one of the good guys."

"You just keep chattering," he said. "You're getting on my nerves."

She kept her hands firmly on the wheel but with a glance at Kate. She was surprised to find Kate smiling as if she was enjoying herself. Then Kate began humming the melody of Gilligan's Island. Jodi shook her head in disgust.

Getting away from the dock was easier than she feared. For a while, neither of them could think of anything but getting the sails ready, and then a strong wind caught them, and Kate dropped nimbly down to the deck and gripped a handrail tightly.

It was time.

The lights of the boat glistened off the water, and Jodi heard Kate's soft gasp.

She knew even before she looked that there were dolphins in the water. Usually, bluenose dolphins were thick in the water off the coast around springtime, but the early hurricane had made them scarce. Now, some were back, and their lean bodies cut through the water with ease.

"Dolphins are going with us," Jodi told Petak. "Take a look."

He looked over the side and then backed away. His face had gotten a little pale, sickly, but the gun didn't waver in his hand.

Jodi turned the wheel slightly and the boat met a wave head on. The boat bounced violently. She eased it back around again. Bede swallowed and looked down at deck. He shivered. She turned and hit another wave and the Gypsy shuddered. So did Bede. He did not look well. He was a little green.

"Let's dance," Jodi shouted.

She turned the boat almost sideways to the waves and it was a little like being in a car going over railroad tracks. The Gypsy was an old, cranky boat and every part of her seemed to move up and down with each wave.

Bede stepped away from the side and rested his back against the cabin door. He was even more pale.

"You remember that hamburger place they used to have on Macklin Street, Kate?" Jodi asked.

Kate glanced at Bede's sickly-looking face. "Oh yes. That was the one where you used to get the steak sandwich and onion rings. You said they were so good because they never changed the grease in the fryer."

Bede made a gagging sound.

"You couldn't get their onion rings for take-out," Jodi said. "The grease would eat through the bag by the time you got it home."

"Shut up," Bede said weakly. "Both of you. Shut up. Stop talking about food."

"What should we talk about then" Jodi asked. "It's a long trip to Florida."

Bede sank down on the Gypsy's deck, but he still pointed the gun.

"I don't want to talk about anything," he said weakly.

"Would you have really married her?" Jodi asked.

"It doesn't matter now," he said.

Jodi turned the Gypsy slightly, felt the heavy old boat coming more alive under her toes. The speed was picking up, movement more violent.

She thought she was done with ghosts and she was not expecting it when the shimmering figure of Donna appeared next to Bede. For the first time her face was complete. Her large eyes were sad, and Jodi understood how pretty she must have been in life.

"He killed me," she said. "Bede killed me."

Donna looked shocked.

Jodi wondered why Donna had never really appeared as solidly as Timothy, but perhaps it would be better to worry about that when somebody wasn't pointing a gun at her.

A particularly nasty wave nearly turned the Gypsy sideways. Even Jodi was not prepared. It took her a few seconds to get the boat back under control, and by then Bede was being violently ill. He still held on to the pistol but both Jodi and Kate knew how weak a person was when they were so seasick. Kate took a few steps and lifted the gun easily from his fingers.

She held it gingerly out to Jodi and Jodi stuffed it into the side pocket of her jacket. Jodi eased the big boat around and headed back.

No more dancing on the waves.

"Have you ever been seasick?" Kate asked.

"I don't remember if I was," Jodi answered. "Would you get on the radio and call Dad. He's probably pretty worried."

She only half-listened to Kate calling the marina, because Donna was still hovering. She expected Donna to be angry at

Bede for killing her, but instead she moved close and patted Bede comfortingly on the shoulder. Jodi wondered if there was some part of Bede who could feel it. Donna left Bede and seemed to float across the deck to Jodi.

"I wish..." she said.

She never got to say what she wished for she started becoming transparent just as Timothy had done, and finally she was only a shimmering outline, and then vapor. The vapor seemed to move out over the water and then vanished beneath the waves.

Kate stepped back to the wheel.

"Your dad called the Sheriff's department. They'll all be waiting. Geoffrey Hamilton will be waiting too."

"Oh?"

"Bud said he must have been listening to the police ban radio, and he called as soon as he heard the sheriff's guys were on their way to the Marina. Bud said he sounded very concerned."

"Oh?" Jodi said again.

"Are you okay?" Kate asked.

"I'm fine," Jodi said.

"It's that you're even paler than normal. You look like you've seen a ghost."

Kate looked a little alarmed when Jodi started to laugh.

Made in the USA
Monee, IL
03 February 2020

21243529R00129